STORIES
FROM THE EDGE
OF THE SEA

· · · · · · · · · ·

Andrew Lam

 Red Hen Press | *Pasadena, CA*

Book design by Mark E. Cull.

Library of Congress Cataloging-in-Publication Data

Names: Lam, Andrew, author.
Title: Stories from the edge of the sea / Andrew Lam.
Description: First edition. | Pasadena, CA: Red Hen Press, 2025.
Identifiers: LCCN 2024043138 (print) | LCCN 2024043139 (ebook) | ISBN 9781636282428 (paperback) | ISBN 9781636282435 (ebook)
Subjects: LCGFT: Short stories.
Classification: LCC PS3612.A54328 S76 2025 (print) | LCC PS3612.A54328 (ebook) | DDC 813/.6—dc23/eng/20240924
LC record available at https://lccn.loc.gov/2024043138
LC ebook record available at https://lccn.loc.gov/2024043139

The National Endowment for the Arts, the Los Angeles County Arts Commission, the Ahmanson Foundation, the Dwight Stuart Youth Fund, the Max Factor Family Foundation, the Pasadena Tournament of Roses Foundation, the Pasadena Arts & Culture Commission and the City of Pasadena Cultural Affairs Division, the City of Los Angeles Department of Cultural Affairs, the Audrey & Sydney Irmas Charitable Foundation, the Meta & George Rosenberg Foundation, the Albert and Elaine Borchard Foundation, the Adams Family Foundation, Amazon Literary Partnership, the Sam Francis Foundation, and the Mara W. Breech Foundation partially support Red Hen Press.

First Edition
Published by Red Hen Press
www.redhen.org

With wit and tenderness, Andrew Lam consistently subverts conventions familiar to diasporic literature. Humor, linguistic virtuosity and wholly originally voices abound in *Stories from the Edge of the Sea's* tightly crafted narratives.

—Paul Christiansen, editor of *Saigoneer* magazine,
  and author of *Beneath Saigon's Chò Nâu*

In this personal collection of stories, Andrew Lam bathes readers in a soup of memory. From Vietnamese wartime villas to college flats in Berkeley, we taste the desires of comedians, soldiers, tomboys, friends, queers, mothers, and refugees. Lam reveals a loving community where acts of care are savored and stirred to perfection.

—Long Bui, associate professor, Department of Global & International Studies, UCI, and author of *Returns of War: South Vietnam and the Price of Refugee Memory*

Andrew Lam was one of the first voices to emerge from the astonishing crash of literature from the first, second, and now third generation of Vietnamese-American writers and poets that has graced and become an integral part of the American canon, and in this collection, he continues to cement his place as a leading figure in that literature. The stories, as the title promises, touch from the sea's western edge that marked the departure of the thousands of Vietnamese refugees to America, to its eastern border, the Land's End that was the land's beginning for them—and specifically San Francisco, Andrew Lam's city, the city most on the edge of the future. Lam takes us into the lives of the new generations, torn between cultures, adapting or battered or victorious in the new world of start-ups or drive-bys, of the LGBTQ choices natural to a new generation but a source of tension or secrecy with their parents, of the eternal decision of what to hang onto and what to let go. How we live now is always a great theme of literature, and Lam, as a great writer must do, finds new and contemporary forms to meet that task. He cleverly brings a modern idiom to his stories—there are tales told as Facebook entries, or in a stand-up comedians' monologue—but he never lets cleverness replace their core humanity: he manages to mix raunchy humor with gentle wisdom or with tragic poignancy. I laughed out loud reading of a model minority student who exoticizes his refugee past only to be subsumed by it, or of the disparate lives somehow threaded by pho soup; a story which includes careful and tender instructions of how to prepare that miracle food—but it was a laughter that always stemmed from or came to an acknowledgment of pain, a pain and the strength that pain gifts people in order to deal with it, epitomized finally in the last piece in the collection: Lam's wonderful and moving and triumphant eulogy of his mother.

—Wayne Karlin, author of *Memorial Days:*
  Việt Nam Stories 1973–2022, A Wolf by the Ears, and other novels

No one maps the moveable feast of the Vietnamese diaspora like Andrew Lam. From standup comedians to social chameleons, from college student strivers to lovelorn lawyers taking a strip-tease walk on the wild side, Lam's characters feel like old friends with shocking secrets to unfold—forced to confront the lost country of the human heart.

—Scott Lankford, Professor of English (emeritus), Foothill College,
  Los Altos Hills, CA, author of *Tahoe Beneath the Surface*

*For my niece, Amy Lam, who passed much too soon,
but who blesses us still with her love.*

Contents

Foreword

Many years ago in northern Laos, I witnessed a soul-retrieving ritual to heal a sick woman, and it left an enduring impression. Villagers at the foot of a mountain had gathered in a circle and in the middle danced a handsome young man in traditional Hmong garb with an equally colorful rooster in his arms, which he raised high above his head. Accompanying him was an old shaman wearing a red hood that covered his face. He shook a ring full of coins as he trembled and chanted while others blew elegiac notes on buffalo horns and bamboo flutes, and yet a few more banged gongs and sang.

All about me incense smoke drifted.

The ritual? To appease the dead and retrieve fragments of a sick woman's soul, or so my guide told me. He pointed to a young woman who sat listlessly between two older ones on a bamboo bench nearby, their arms on her back, supporting her. All three were wearing black traditional Hmong clothing with colorful trimmings and headdresses.

The young woman was in love, but the man she loved had died suddenly, and illness took her. "He took parts of her with him," said my guide.

Hence the soul retrieval ritual. And it required a blood sacrifice.

In solemn gestures, the young dancer placed the bird on the ground. Others knelt down to help. They spoke to the bird. It was asked to fly to the spirit world to retrieve scattered fragments of the young woman's soul. The feathers from its neck were plucked, more horns blown. One of the older men placed a black ceramic bowl under it. The young man took out a switch blade from his pocket. And cut.

The rooster kicked and jerked. I closed my eyes. I felt heady. The heat, the noise, and the trekking earlier that morning had taken their toll. I sat on the ground, but I felt that somehow I, too, was traveling on the bird's wings.

How would the friendly tour guide know that I was no different than that young woman? I, too, was suffering from a broken heart. Though as a journalist I traveled the world and filed reports, I felt that I was never going to be whole again.

Afterward, during lunch, I asked my guide, "Wonder if the ritual worked?" And he laughed. "Not sure. But it seems to make everyone feel better. That's all you can do, right?" Then he asked, not expecting an answer: "Is there a magic that can heal heartbreaks?"

Many years have flown by since that moment. I am no shaman, and I've got no magic spells. All I've got are my imagination and the desire to tell stories. I know I can never retrieve what is lost. But I am determined at least to try to heal—to retrieve those fragments as best as I can—one story at a time.

STORIES FROM THE EDGE OF THE SEA

"Love is wandering in the labyrinth of your heart without a fucking map, is lust is lost is hurt is endless longing, baby . . . love is luv . . ."

—*Overheard from a young man nursing his single malt near the end of happy hour.*

"Tell me, is there a romance that lasts?"

—*My mother in the garden of her retirement home before Alzheimer's took her tongue.*

She in a Dance of Frenzy

She grew up a tomboy, could swing a bat the way her younger brother couldn't, could kick the glasses off a guy's face, and was not, therefore, very close to her mother. Mother with her gossip and her housewifery chores and her hidden gambling debts and her heavy-set body was never interesting to her, was never outdoorsy, was too much involved with the family things to see the world, the ocean, for instance, the blue sky.

She, the tomboy who laughed and played, on the other hand, liked sports, liked kung fu movies, liked sparring, liked to be liked, liked men.

She especially liked hanging out with her Papa, once a sergeant in the South Vietnamese Marine Corps, a trained assassin during the war, or something dangerous like that, though she was too young in that country to remember for sure. It didn't matter, really. All she knew was that he was a gentle man. From him, she learned how to hook worms, how to cast, how to be silent so the fish would come. She learned from Papa to move with the rhythm of the ocean, feeling the boat bobbing this way and that, learned to appreciate his solitude; the old man was sometimes like a stone statue, an ancient being perhaps, yet if a fish was caught, would become so vigorously alive.

So scrawny and thin and small, who would have ever thought she, the tomboy, was going to become a beautiful woman?

But then at sixteen, she bled. And the blood oozed out of her like a stream of snapdragons and daffodils. A late bloomer, everyone commented, and late bloomers last forever. So beautiful, so elegant; grew breasts and ass and grew hair so long and dark and silky, possessing a smile that dazzled and the agility of a gazelle and the breathlessness of a dove in flight.

At a dinner party thrown for her father's fiftieth birthday, all the men were trying hard not to look when she served them drinks. "That couldn't be her!" they kept saying, and her father laughed and said, "It is! It is! My little tomboy."

One man, the youngest among her father's army buddies, now a successful real estate broker and recently divorced, openly flirted with her. "Marry me," he said, "you're the most beautiful thing on earth!"

"Sure, Uncle, any time," she said and sat on his lap the way she used to when she was younger, "and I want you to buy me a castle up in the hills!"

"Anything!" he said. "Anything, my princess," and they all laughed, but she saw her father's eyes trained on her for half a second. She's my little tomboy, her father said to his friends again, and she said, of course, Papa, always, you know that. But afterward, when the men were gone, her father slapped her. You acted like a whore, he said, but she heard echoing in that slap her father's friend's departing whisper—You're so fuckin' gorgeous!—and almost laughed out loud.

So fuckin' gorgeous that her beauty turned into a curse, no longer fitting in the way she used to in her own home, how she moved in her crowded house was all different now, so fuckin' gorgeous that an unspoken tension between her and her sisters, who were not gorgeous, grew, so fuckin' gorgeous that her brothers averted their gaze upon her approach and stopped sparring with her, so fuckin' gorgeous that her mother grew more cold and distant, so fuckin' gorgeous that, at seventeen, she fled.

It was time, in any case, for her to see the world. Quietly, she packed her bags and afterward said goodbye to her family, and they protested, but she wondered if the females of the household weren't secretly a little happy to see her leave.

They wept, and she wept, but away she went. To college in the North where she met a man and then another man and then another. In fact, men of all sorts and all kinds of colors and stripes flocked to her. Men so strong and young and sensual and handsome and intelligent and ambitious, rich and poor men. Men who fell in love with her and she, she thought, with them. She had all the grace in the world. Intelligent and possessing a vivid imagination, exciting and fun, and she could dance the cha-cha-cha, do the pasodoble and tango on a whim. She could stretch her legs effortlessly the way a swan stretched its snowy wings and would smile and coo as a lover entered her, and she, when it rained, could sigh with a profundity that made poetry worthwhile—wouldn't she make a wonderful companion to any man, an extraordinary wife to the son of a bitch who happened to win her heart?

But where, pray tell, was her heart? Strange, but she would always feel unattached to these men afterward, always feeling alone, unhappy, and the sex and the embrace were only fleeting moments, and the men and their beauty and their talents and their future evaporated with the wind or were swept away by the rain and the fog that drifted down from the hills in the early morning.

Her girlfriend would ask, how is it going with so and so? And she would sigh and say rather vaguely, Oh, it's all right, but . . .

But it was not all right. She grew bored easily and would find faults in these men, because of course they, being only men, all have faults.

You know I don't like roses . . .

But it wasn't because of their faults that her relationships with them didn't last. It was something else deep inside her, something that forced her to close her eyes or groan aloud, something that made her fear that her relationships would and would not last, which became, after a while, the same thing. And so, one by one, she left them, or they her.

"What's the matter, honey," one of the men asked. "Did I do something wrong?"

"Nothing's the matter, sweetie," she said, sighing, "maybe it's just the weather. Maybe it's just us being too comfortable with each other." And soon his heart was broken: she did not want to see him again.

"We are just friends," she would say to one, or, "Our relationship has deviated and now we are brother and sister," to another. And soon another heart was broken. Then another. Then another.

So many that she decided to do away with the noise of their hearts shattering in her answering machine. She disconnected the phone, gave away the machine that recorded the sounds of broken hearts, and while she was at it, cleared away cobwebs and debris in her apartment, threw out a table, a futon, two chairs, and all the boxer shorts and ties and shirts that had accumulated in her closet. Ah, there now, the peace, this space, this solitude, she said to herself afterward, this is what I crave. From now on, it's just me and myself.

Yet the sadness continued. And soon, out of loneliness, she had a new lover and reconnected the phone, and some of the broken hearts continued to crash in the tape, and some were done with their shattering and could be heard no more. But, really, who was counting? Not her. She remained unhappy and distant, and the fog continued to drift some mornings past her apartment, and already she wanted to flee from this new lover, a tall and handsome light-skinned African American, a bouncer studying to be a filmmaker, but she resisted because she knew the routine would restart all over and she was beyond tired.

But what was the matter with her? Was she cursed by someone, a water witch maybe, the kind popular in Vietnamese folklore, to live the rest of her life in a pallid light?

She could find no answer for these questions because life had become a little blurry now, the way her audience appeared to her when she danced at this upscale strip bar and restaurant. But if she could just work, doing what she did well, a little dancing, a little flirting, a little flaunting of her exquisite flesh, maybe something else would emerge. Maybe if she went away again to some faraway place, maybe if she changed her apartment and had more sunlight, or maybe if she took up the offer of that young rich customer and flew to Paris on his private jet, or consented to go to Hollywood with the fat one and ride in his limousine and watch how he made fantasies come true, maybe it would solve some of her mysterious angsts.

Maybe . . .

Late one night after coming back from dancing, she stepped out of a long hot bath, and her favorite green towel fell from her hair and onto the floor. As she stooped to pick it up, something in the pattern of the crumpled fabric caused her to feel immense nausea and she, in a panic, fled to her bedroom to bury her face in her down pillows.

She began to see faces, some well-known and some belonging to complete strangers. They crowded about her in a very dark room, and she felt as if she were drowning. Then, faintly, she heard waves lapping against the side of a boat. Someone was calling out her name, her Vietnamese name. She tried to locate that voice from those sad faces in that crowded room, and it was confusing at first. But slowly, she recognized the one that was calling out to her. It was a face she knew at a time before she became a beautiful woman and a dancer, before she spoke English and before America. It was, of course, her father's face, and it came to her as she slept on this mat in the hull of this boat full of refugees in the middle of the Pacific, a tiny tot she was and dying of thirst. Her family was about her, and the air was humid and fetid, and a strange drowsiness was the curse on everyone's eyes. Her father said, "Wake up, little one, wake up and drink this milk before you die."

She remembered how the sun was bearing down on her and how the wind was blowing stronger now and remembered seeing out of the corner of her eyes how blue the ocean was, how vast. Then she felt her father lifting her toward him, and she tasted again that sticky warm liquid, and the world entered her through those few meager gulps. She looked up to her father then and blinked and even tried to smile, for deep down, she knew she would survive, if only just for him.

And now in her bed, now a young beauty weeping, she knew that she was most happy then and not now. For there could be nothing truer than her father's gesture at that moment and everything else—

America, the men who loved her, who cared, who wept, who danced, whose hearts shattered like crystals in her answering machine, even the happy home from which she fled, even Paris and Hollywood and limousines and cold hard cash were a poor metaphor for what she desired. What she craved was that fleeting gesture on that ocean, now more than ever, felt that frenzied thirst welling up from deep inside her, a thirst so potent, so exquisitely all-consuming that nothing in this world, not even love, could hope to quench it.

Agape at the Guggenheim

Yo Journal!

Long time no write. I know, I know. I'm lousy at this on-a-regular thing. Keeping a notebook is good for wannabe writers. I read Didion's essay, so I know. I know.

Still, since I am drinking, and words are flowing, Journey, here it goes. A doozy, I promise.

Two long lines for tickets at the Guggenheim this morning, I stood in one; in the other, a nervous Romeo—his chestnut Polo clings lovingly to his lean, mean torso.

The crowd: maximum capacity. *China's 5,000 Years of Civilization* was on display, and it seemed every New Yorker was a Sinophile this Sunday morn. A summer torrent had just passed. The Gug, despite the air-conditioning, felt like a steam bath.

He kept stealing glances at me. I kept stealing them back. He'd rolled up the pamphlet in his hand and twirled it like a drumstick around his dexterous fingers, and my heart was a tom-tom waiting for his drum-drum-a-drumming. I pretended to read mine. But Journo dear, not a tom-tom- a tom-tom . . .-word got through.

Then, like synchronized swimmers, we both wiped our foreheads with the palms of our hands, and this most innocent yet serendipitous gesture caused us to look at each other and smile.

That smile. Those eyes. They evaporated the muggy day. I'd gone in search of my ancestral roots (yes, I will admit, *entre nous,* my paternal grandfather was Chinese!) before flying back to California on the morrow, but what did I find today instead? Adonis loved by lust auroral.

Alabaster skin, muscular arms, blushed cheeks, curly hair clinging strategically on his smooth forehead. I wondered: what does he see when he looks at me? Previews of Terracotta Warriors waiting for him on the second floor? Shy Asian boy starving for love? Brunch?

Our lines moved at different tempos, alas. He got his ticket before me as my line limped at tortoise pace. Though he dawdled at the entrance to Frank L. Wright's famous spiral stairwell, the crowd surged and pulled and soon crested my man upward, away from view.

I grew more anxious with each minute. Time dragggggged on. Finally, with ticket in hand, I rushed after him. But it was not to be. A big surly guard with a beer belly stood between me and Romance.

"You have to check in your umbrella," he growled.

"I do? Why?"

"It's-the-rule," he enunciated each word, his arms spread out as if Christ on a cross. "The-umbrella-line-starts-over-there. *Comprendes*?"

Journal, for some reason Enormous Ignoramus seemed to think that anyone who is non-white speaks Spanish. If only Señor *No Educado* would turn around, he might see what he was supposed to be guarding: five thousand years of sophistication and intricate craftwork and profound poetry etched on stone, gilded in gold, painted onto porcelain—yes, by people who did not a word of English speak. Sadly, *el matón no entiende nada.*

I would have loved to tell beefy guard what he could do with my lacquered handle umbrella, but it was a very expensive gift from an admirer.

Listen, Bonjourno, be warned: if you carried an umbrella to see *China's 5,000 Years of Civilization* at the Guggenheim, make sure to add an extra millennium. Be patient, I told myself as I waited in another line. Be calm. Breathe in, find tranquility. Breathe out, find peace.

Think sweet Mama lighting incense and praying to dead ancestors and Lady Quan Yin. Think of Papa spending twelve years in a reeducation camp writing his book of poetry on banana leaves and, when they rotted, memorizing them in his head. Think of the Dalai Lama laughing when asked about suffering. Think of the Laughing Buddha. Think of Thich-Nhat-Hanh, that famed monk from my homeland who spoke English with that haughty Vietnamese-French accent, saying something like: "There's no vay to (h)appiness—(h) appiness is de vay."

But if there is such thing as happiness, surely it's hidden somewhere behind Adonis's shy smile, who must have reached the Late Qing dynasty while I stood in another line, and even as I thought of all the Buddhas and human suffering due to their worldly attachments, my body ached—still aches!—for him, his round butt.

Twenty-five minutes later, I was in. Freed finally from the cursed queues, I spiraled up the Gug in search of my pamphlet-twirling, ivory-teeth-sparkling hero. Thus, three millennia worth of China's ancient civilization streaked and blurred from the corners of my eyes. A blur and a streak. A tom-tom looking for a drumstick. I ran past Liao and Song, hardly notice Zhu, and though I did pause for Tang to admire a few fab brush paintings, I quickly squeezed past Sui to finally arriving at Ming and Qing. Adonis, alas, was nowhere to be seen.

I wanted to see him again so desperately, dear Journo, that I got a headache. Blood pulsed in my veins like thick lava. Throbbed, my temples throbbed.

And what a crowd! People—they jostled, they pushed. They circled statues and gawked at scrolls.

Nasal voice: "Honey, you look a little like this Buddha. You've got his tummy!"

Baritone: "Marge, look at this. What a pearl! Size of a golf ball."

Shrill: "Bob, look at that crown. Gotta weigh a ton!"

Journey dear, New York Chinatown on a Saturday morning was vastly more orderly.

When a lady bumped her sizable derriere into me as she leaned down to study three rather Rubenesque white porcelain fairies in a glass cage, I almost tumbled backward into the arms of a terra-cotta warrior, who looked at me and the crowd slightly annoyed. And I imagine, given the humidity, would have preferred being interred to being gawked at.

The fairies: they were holding each other's hands while standing on a porcelain boat. Their faces round, expressive. The last one, whose head was cracked a little on the side, reminded me of my antique-loving mother, forehead creased slightly with concerns, as if in rebuke (despite the smile), Son, how could you possibly skip Song?

I felt a presence behind me then, a particular heat on my back, and turned.

Up close, he was even more spectacular. Emerald eyes with gold tints at the rim. A faint but intoxicating musk emanated from his torso.

In my mind, a dozen scenarios blossomed, one in which Adonis and I fall in love, we build a life together in a duplex on the seizième or roosting in an atelier rustic, and one on the Rive Gauche in the sixth (with a little balcony where we have coffee in blue porcelain bowls in the morning and I get to butter his baguette).

He draws or sculpts—but does not, I repeat, does not, write poetry, please, we know how that went—and me, well, I'll be a genuine writer instead of a low-life paralegal.

You Tarzan, me Boy. You chisel, me scribble.

But I didn't say a word. His beauty robbed me of my tongue. He was about to say something when a throng of elderly women pushed themselves between us New York style to look at the Princess Dowager's pearl-studded crown at the corner, and we were forced apart once more.

A man's loud voice rang out: "Keep moving, folks! Keep moving! Please, we're at maximum capacity. Please! Keep moving!" And so just like that, Adonis was swept away again with the crowd, and the spell thus broken.

I tried to follow. I did. But a few tall shoulders and a few over-coiffed hairpieces later, lost sight of him I did. The Gug started to feel like Dante's Inferno, albeit a few circles short.

So, this a Lysander conundrum: what course of true love ever smoothly runs? Even in such a lovely, well-designed spiral-ramped building topped by a large skylight.

In my case, Journal, love's path was twirled upward through a labyrinth made of sweaty and unpleasant humans amidst dazzling Chinese antiquities. Hell, indeed, is other people.

For the next hour, I sought and searched. To no avail, alas, nary a sigh from my lover heard.

Finally on the fifth floor, I stopped and sat down to massage my calves. When I looked up, I found myself in a room full of Buddha statues from the various dynasties. The Buddhas, standing in meditation, sitting in lotus position, lying on their sides with eyes closed in serenity, all seemed to be half-smiling knowingly. The one nearest me was a sensuous looking statue in a lotus position, with his hand raised, showing me the simple lines of his palm, the other arm outstretched, finger touching the ground. He offered a half smile. Like a smirk.

That touch . . . that gesture . . .

Deeply moved, I stepped back, clasped my hands together. Journal, I was surprised by what I did next. With eyes closed, yes, I started to pray like that pious child I used to be.

I have not prayed in front of a Buddha since I came to America more than twenty years ago, mind you. I was but six going on seven, and that was the last time. Old enough to remember praying with mother for a million things. We prayed for the war to end, then later for my father to be released from that infernal commie gulag, for me to receive good grades, and secretly I prayed for my mother to remain beautiful forever and always be by my side.

Buddha never granted me any of these wishes, except that the war did end, but it ended so badly. My family and I fled out to sea. My father died a year after his release back home, a broken man in a broken shed, long before we could possibly sponsor him over. And my mother, who is still beautiful, but whose hair turned gray overnight after his death, is now estranged from me—she can't handle the gay thing, being so pious—so I stopped praying.

But this morning, years after I had given up talking to the dead ancestors and all the Buddhas, years after I have moved on from one language to another, having changed my name and allegiance, I started to pray at the Guggenheim.

Why? 'Cause, (this is between us, ok?) I felt so alone.

What did I pray for? I prayed to see him again. That's it.

I don't know why I felt that I had to, though I had given up the chase. Soon after that, deflated, I weaved my way downstream and retrieved my lacquer-handled umbrella.

It had stopped raining. So I decided to walk. I strolled through Central Park, where water dripped dropped from the tree branches onto the muddy ground forming reflecting puddles of the silvery sky. Mindlessly, I walked. And walked. I walked until my right knee hurt, aching from that old skiing accident in Tahoe. Still, Journ-o, I couldn't stop-o. I limped a little, slouching toward Bethlehem, a.k.a. the Upper West Side. By the time I crossed the park, it started raining again. I was drenched. Water and sweat dripped-dripped, dropped-dropped from my hair, my brows, my chin.

Images of Adonis smiling kept rising up now and then, but by the time I got to Manhattan Ave, it was now mixed with real hunger. I hadn't gotten anything in me but a cup of cappuccino in the early morn.

I kept walking, limping on Manhattan then Columbus Ave, and by some odd impulse found myself veering left down Amsterdam toward downtown. I was by now drenched and the umbrella now a bonafide walking stick. Click, click, click, so went its tip on the sidewalk. I had an inkling of a clock ticking, and as I trudged, I had a vision of myself in old age shuffling toward death, bound by this impossible yearning for love, yes, till that melancholic end.

Click. Click. Click. Click.

I didn't know where I was going exactly, I just kept on walking, my leather shoes soaked through.

Click. Click. Click.

When I went further south and walked into a French bistro for lunch, my feet felt leaden. I ordered *moules et frites* and a Grey Goose martini, extra dirty.

I sat next to the window. But it was all steamed up from the humidity. It was impossible to see the street outside. So, impulsively, I stood up, and in one fluid, expressive stroke, wiped an uninhibited full circle from that misty pane.

The world outside sparkled. The street glimmered with the sun now peeking out like a bright pearl sitting over an oyster bed of a nimbus.

So . . . here's the kicker, Journal Dear.

Strolling down the sidewalk across the street, I see a familiar figure.

I squinted. I knitted brows.

No! Can't be.

Yes! Can. Can be.

We were miles from the Guggenheim. Yet there he walked, down Amsterdam Ave, looking into store windows, taking his time. He was rained on, too. But the rain made him even more beautiful, his skin glowing, the shirt still on him jealously clinging. And the pamphlet he once twirled now hung limply from his back pocket (I had lost mine).

My first impulse? To run out, to greet. If I could muster it, I'd tell him that I found him insanely beautiful. I would ask him to join me for lunch. And maybe for his hand in marriage.

But just like that another impulse rose up, and it told me to sit my ass back down. And I gave in to the latter.

Journal—through that circle on an otherwise fogged-up pane, I stared, mouth agape.

What is this thing in me that wants to pick up and go, to chase, and then after the chase, evade? This impulse that moves me across continents, oceans, to be elsewhere, to meet another? Then there's this yearning that's completely opposite: to sit still and breathe in and out and be mindful, to find solitude—I mean, what's up with that?

I sat in admiration before all the serene Buddhas on their lotus flowers, but why was my heart beating a mile a minute?

I saw the future then, saw that this longing doesn't end; it stays in the heart as long as it beats. And it keeps governing my grief, yet it's also clear that it feeds my imagination. Knowing this, I had to close my eyes lest I cry and scare the waiter.

Then guess what I saw with eyes closed? Yup, those three plump fairies laughing hysterically on their porcelain boat.

So I laughed with them.

I mean, laughter seemed the only proper response, a moment so free—free of everything—until the waiter showed up to refill my water glass, scowling.

"Sir, is there anything else you want?"

"No. Not a thing."

Omm Omm Omm—ohm my god that dude was *so* cute.

I breathed in, breathed out.

After the longest of sighs, probably the longest in my life, to all the Buddhas with sensuous arms and delicate fingers and mysterious smiles, to mindfulness and to mindless lust, to Adonis's roan back, which had just glimpsed out of view, I, dear Journey, I raised my half-full, extra dirty martini, in praise.

This Isle Is Full of Noises

One bright afternoon, on a small, unnamed island in the Gulf of Thailand, a scrawny boy climbs to the top of a sand dune, lies down, then gawks at the sky. Bright clouds drift slowly by; the ocean roars in his ears. A small thunderstorm had passed that morning, but already the sand is burning hot.

Down the beach, fifty yards or so, a small crowd gathers over a newly marked grave, one of a dozen neatly lining the beach. A plank from a fishing boat, whose skeleton exposed and battered near shore can be seen lying listless at a distance, serves as tombstone. A young woman, supported by two older ones, is crying into the crook of her elbow.

The boy continues to stare upward. He hears footsteps on the sand but does not turn. "Catfish in mango sauce," says the approaching boy, who lies down next to him. "You see it too?"

"Of course," he answers, though he doesn't. "And the one on the left, roast chicken in lemongrass and chili pepper."

"I see that!" his friend agrees. "But look over there. That's shrimp paste wrapped in sugarcane."

"No!" says the boy rather loudly as he props himself up on his elbow to look into his friend's eyes. "Wrong! Wrong! I've been looking at it." His voice softens as he looks back up to the sky; it's as if he's been waiting for the cloud to open and drop its hidden treasures upon him. "Ice cream cone with three scoops," he says with conviction. "Did you know there are thirty-one flavors of ice cream in America? Only America has that. That's what they say, thirty-one flavors, can you imagine?"

• • • •

The sun is setting over the rice paddies. The water reflects gold and silver under waving, ripening blades. A GI stands looking down at a dying teenager curling in a fetal position at his boots, his torso bleeding from three bullet wounds. Other GIs mill about looking tired and nervous. His teeth kicked out, the teenager's scrawny face is a smear of saliva and blood. He gurgles inaudible words. The wind rustles leaves, stirs elephant grass and rice blades. The sounds of a chopper whirl overhead, getting louder. Sporadic distant gunfire resounds like firecrackers.

Nelson, let's go.

No. Not yet.

The GI leans down.

Under blue sky, the knife in his hand flashes like a flame.

• • • •

A breezy October morning, when the leaves have turned on the UC Berkeley campus, Cao Le Y-Bang, a.k.a. Koala, prances down the steps of the Life Science Building, clutching his biochem midterm like a deed to a gold mine. Landing on the lawn, he folds the exam, clenches it between his teeth like a bit, drops his backpack, and somersaults backward several times as three appreciative female students underneath a fluttering willow look on.

Scrawled on the upper right-hand corner of his midterm's front page is Professor Jenkins's comment:

"93/100—Good job, Mr. Cao!
beats you-know-who with the
highest score."

Koala reads it as a kind of haiku—a haiku that'd send him to med school, that is. Sweeter still, he beat you-know-who. Even with his "special advantage," he does not expect in a class of 154 bright and competitive students, plus a couple of geniuses among them, the highest score. The highest score traditionally belongs to Bryan Cox, or Cocky Bryan, as Koala likes to call him. A legend in Organic Chem 8A and 8B, Bryan Cox attended college at sixteen and can reproduce the periodic table and the Kreb's cycle in his sleep. But that same morning, Cox, who majors in English and only minors in biochem, now in his second year, is watching his unseeded competitor tumbling on the lawn with suspicion.

When Koala spots his nemesis, he vamps it up. A victory dance: doing a roundhouse kick, he imagines kicking Cocky Bryan's inflated ego to pieces. Doing his favorite kata, blocking and chopping, he sees himself defeating his invisible enemies as he makes his way toward the grand prize: Stanford med school.

The girls applaud as Koala bows in an exaggerated flourish. "Here, catch!" says the girl in the middle as she tosses a golden apple toward him. It flies in a high arc above his head, but Koala jumps and deftly catches it. He removes his spit-moistened exam between his clenched teeth, turns sideways to look at Cocky Bryan, who still studies him, and takes a crunchy, hearty bite. Sweet!

Koala, who subsists on a combination of scholarships and work-study programs, has struggled very hard to stay within the top twentieth percentile. The frat boy, on the other hand, led every class they had together with ease.

Was it only a few weeks ago that he had nightmares over Jenkins's notorious midterm, one dubbed by many who took his course as "The Sphinx's Riddle"? If he doesn't ace this class, his chance of getting into Stanford will be seriously jeopardized. But "for every difficult situation," or so his father had often told him in Vietnamese, "you'll find a good strategy to solve it. Focus on it and you'll find the opportunity and take the path. Trust your instincts."

As far as advice goes, it was vague and mysterious, something left surely from the old man's tribal hunting memories when he was still a child in Vietnam's central highlands, using crossbows and arrows. Nevertheless, Koala took it to heart. Over time he refashioned it into something like a guiding principle.

From that equation, Koala learned to find his own path in life and to develop strategies for every difficult situation. His motto since junior high is to be "badass on the street, but kick-ass in school."

So, strategy: endure Jenkins's office hours twice a week, bond with him if possible. "I hope to gain insight into the Sphinx's mind," he boasted to his girlfriend, Darma Penotiere, one afternoon while sitting on the stone steps of Wheeler Hall—to which Bryan Cox, affecting his trademark nonchalance, commented as he walked by, "Or find out what's on the freaking test."

Darma laughed at the comment but gripped Koala's tensed arm at the same time so he wouldn't stand up. "One does what one must to get past the Sphinx, darling," she quipped. Koala, stunned, only managed to give his nemesis's back the birdie. "Now, now," said Darma, then kissed his cheek and held onto to his arm until Cox had turned a corner, "a smile recures the wounding of a frown."

He hated Shakespeare's funky, sissy-like English. Still, Koala wasn't aware that he was frowning. It didn't help that Darma flirted with Cox when he was being insulted. He tried to swallow his anger. He was a student at Berkeley now, he told himself, a lot was riding on him. Had this occurred back in his neighborhood in West Oakland and among his posse, honor would demand that Koala, who, though a scholarship boy, competed in high school gymnastics and had a black belt in karate to boot, kick the wuss's ass.

• • • •

Of all those regularly attending the Sphinx's office hours, Koala did have one thing in his favor. The professor, when he was young and had more hair, was a passionate anti-war protester. That experience more or less colored his politics. Jenkins, rumored to have been nominated for the Nobel Prize for his research involving enzymes that spliced DNA into fragments and then reattached the strands in ingenious ways, took an immediate liking to Koala, someone he once referred to as America's "Cold War Victim." With uncharacteristic animation,

Jenkins, whose number was high on the draft, had boasted of his own participation in the peace movement, a movement that, according to his assessment, eventually ended "that atrocious war."

If DNA splicing lectures weren't boring enough, Jenkins's history lessons bored him even more. But Koala was also vaguely alarmed. He kept nodding while a need to take a different view nagged at him. Taking his late father's position was difficult, however. His inarticulate father, who fought in the Vietnam War alongside the Americans, but in America drank and smoked himself to death, never communicated his ideas in depth. The gist: America abandoned their allies in the middle of a battlefield, an untrustworthy ally, and an unreliable friend when the chips were down. But Koala had very little to rely upon, being too young to have any memories of that war, and too busy with school and karate to keep himself from getting beaten up to really give a fuck. Now, of course, it was all too late.

He didn't want to sound ill-informed though. So, strategy: resort to telling Jenkins personal history instead, reciting his own statement in the college application—e.g., how hard it was to be a boy from a disadvantaged economic circumstance and struggling to do well in a poor neighborhood school with a widowed mother who does nails for a living, and how well he did, having graduated cum laude from high school.

One quiet afternoon in Jenkins's office, when the midterm drew near, that story unexpectedly expanded. Jenkins, having explained the intricacies of ribosomes, asked if Koala wanted a cup of coffee.

"Sure," he said. "Thank you."

He needed it, too; hadn't slept so well, stressed out of his skull. Worse, he studied and studied, but the DNA strands still uncoiled in strange fashions in his dreams. He wasn't getting the full visual grip of the material. Some mornings, he felt sorry for himself. In his bleaker moments, he saw his future as damned as his father's, and that had frightened him more than dying.

As he stared at the hand-painted coffee cup with a single sloop sailing amid a blue ocean, the coffee steam drifting slowly upward, his eyes began to water.

"Something the matter, Mr. Cao?"

Koala looked up. "I'm just reminded of this woman who brought two kilos of coffee beans with her on the boat. She drowned, you know," he heard himself saying.

"Oh?" said Jenkins.

"Like she didn't know if there'd be coffee in America," he said with genuine anger. "A week out to sea, our food's gone and water rationed to half a cup a person, and the crazy woman chewed on the beans then threw up chunks of it into the sea."

Jenkins swallowed. "If it's all right with you, Mr. Cao, if you don't mind, well, I would like to hear the rest of that story."

Koala looked at the Sphinx, saw a path opening before him, and he took it. "All right," he said and asked Jenkins to close the door. In a solemn and sporadically cracked voice, the veins on his temples throbbing, Koala proceeded to paint a dark river that led to a vast moon-lit sea, a crowded boat, the constant bobbing on the waters, the sounds of whispers and muffled cries and of children weeping, the pud-pud kah-pud coughing of the single diesel engine, the fear in his parents' eyes, his little brother's crying under a blue blanket, the subsequent thirst and hunger, pitch black nights, burning blue sky days, the sounds of waves and weeping as his lullabies, the unbearable stench of shit and urine and vomit and the ubiquitous diesel fuel in the crowded, airless haul, the muffled cries for fresh air, for water, for land, and a sea that seemed to stretch forever in every direction; his skin on fire, lips cracked, bleeding.

A terrifying storm sent their boat spinning. People tossed inside the hull, people screaming, vomiting. A few fell overboard and the rest shipwrecked on a near-barren island, one of the Philippines' several thousand. They lived on oysters and mussels pulled from rocks and under sand, feasted on coconuts. They ate boiled kelp, small fish, and tiny crabs. A small spring of fresh water that trickled from moss-covered rocks sustained them. A few months later, when a Filipino trawler saw smoke—they had been burning their clothes and dry coconut shells to attract the boat's attention—and came to their rescue, everyone was skin and bones, near-naked, and scorched by the sun.

But he also remembered playing hide-and-seek, soccer, hopscotch. He remembered catching fish and collecting shells with friends.

More than a hundred people had started out. Only forty-four survived in the end, and among the dead was his younger brother, Truong, the adorable three-year-old who had followed him everywhere like a puppy and who whispered his name the morning he died.

He almost said it again, repeating his own name the way Truong did—Y Bang! Y Bang!—to the biochem professor. But he didn't. Or couldn't. In the dark recess of his mind, the scene of his brother dying in his parents' arms before the storm hit and battered their ship and sent it astray became sacrosanct, and so he glossed over it in the retelling.

He sees it so clearly, as in a newsreel. He sees his father cutting his own index finger and squeezing a few drops of blood into little Truong's gaping mouth. He sees his mother doing the same. He wants to do it too and looks down at his own tiny palm. He raises his hand toward his parents as if to offer his flesh, but no one pays him any attention. And anyway, he is too tired to talk, too thirsty to say what he'd wanted to say. *Cut me! Cut my finger, too!*

His heart quickens; his veins throb. The boat bobs up and down, up and down. His parents' blood drips and drops onto the boy's chin, nose, lips. It's much too late. His brother, suffering from diarrhea and dehydration, whose lips, like everyone else's lips, cracked and bled, is beyond help. All that's recognizable are his wide, trusting eyes, which soon cloud over.

The wind blows stronger now. Dark clouds veil the sun. He sees his father, face sunburnt and eyes stricken with grief, wrap little Truong in a tiny blue blanket. He sees his mother on her knees, weeping in a hoarse, dry voice. He hears his father chant an old song, a hunting song, in the Rade language, a tribal language he does not understand but whose staccato rhythm nevertheless soothes him. His father's lullaby creeps by him, and the others too, who listen, then gathers upon the dark waves, allaying both his sorrow and fury. He sees his father kissing the little boy on the forehead before offering him to the gray, gray sea.

He feels hollowed out every time he thinks of that moment, and almost always, an obstinate rage erupts in him and his body itches as if being pinched by tiny, invisible hands. He can't bear it. Only the memories of his father's chanting, his father's voice, calms him.

Growing up in America, he sometimes tried to convince himself that all of it—the passage out, his brother's death, the shipwreck, and the refugee camps—was a kind of bad dream. Other times, he imagined that it was he who caused the storm, for it seemed to match perfectly his anger and despair. He was only six, after all, when the journey began, an age where magic and reality share a porous border.

Jenkins was very quiet. The professor studied his own palms as if he could read his own future, followed by a teardrop that rolled down the old man's cheek and a quick hand that wiped it away as Koala neared the end of his tale. Surely, the war was being reassessed anew in that brilliant mind of his.

Koala felt mingled with the profound sadness for the loss of little Truong and his father, and the usual if intense and chronic need to put away that wretched past, a muffled sense of triumph welling from deep inside his chest.

• • • •

One cool afternoon in early winter during his first semester, Bryan Cox stops to watch a group of boys playing volleyball in a playground off Bancroft Street; drawn by their laughter, something in their singsong voices stirs an enigmatic yearning within him.

I got it! I got it!

A shirtless boy among them seems to be strutting as much as playing the game, yelling out orders to his teammates, gyrating his hips to the salsa rhythm of the music from a nearby ghetto blaster, touching his mates on their backs, slapping their butts, and high-fiving them whenever they win a point.

A ham. A total ham.

Abruptly, Bryan Cox turns away, the heat rising from his cheeks.

• • • •

Down Telegraph Ave on the wings of doves.

How he figured out Jenkins's questions for the midterm one day during the professor's office hours as the test drew near was, he now feels, part of the right path. Jenkins, in the middle of making coffee, was called away to his laboratory next door during an emergency. Koala went outside to the hall and waited. Jenkins was talking loudly to his two grad students. He mentioned ribosome structures. He wanted his students to intimately know structure; he wanted his students to have a knowledge regarding enzyme splicing and "exons on a single RNA transcript, but occasionally trans-splicing occurs, in which exons on different pre-mRNAs are ligated together. They should know all that."

His problems were solved. He snuck back into the office and opened his biochemistry book and studied. When Jenkins returned a few minutes later and apologized, Koala smiled sweetly. "No problem, sir," he said, even if his heart pounded like a drum. "My pleasure."

Now—the highest score, Mr. Cao!—now, everything had changed. He was smart, but to be better than the rest, all he needed was a nudge in the right direction.

A letter of recommendation from Jenkins was surely in the works. Dr. Martinez, Koala's endocrinology professor, already wrote his. He only needed two more, and plenty of them in the humanities— Kiernan, Rodriguez, Schurmann, or Holt—would write them at the drop of a hat. Really, how could they resist Koala's dimpled smile, his charms, his affectionate yet respectful demeanor, his boy-from-needy-background-striving-to-do-good bio? If he aces the biochem finals and his physics 8B finals, which are difficult but manageable, he can raise his GPA to 3.84, not bad for the most competitive pre-med major in California's best public university.

Koala's imagination begins to race toward the future wherein he'll be fixing failing hearts and faint murmurs, performing triple bypass surgeries and balloon angioplasties, saving fat-assed Americans with blocked arteries from their certain doom. He'll make partner by his mid-thirties, surely with his own practice in his early forties. A house on a cliff with vast UV-reflected windows high above the sea. A blue Porsche parked out in front, a steaming Jacuzzi framed by a mimosa-twined trellis out back.

A wife? Well, green-eyed, redheaded Darma would be a prime candidate, if she doesn't pursue acting. She did taunt him with that domestic possibility: "I always wondered what it would be like to be a doctor's wife," she once said coyly, but it quickened his blood. Anyway, too early to tell. There's still med school, then internship who-knows where. Love will have to wait.

For now, though, the sex is sooo good! He could fuck her three times at one go and still want more. Already she'd hinted at her parents' vacation home in Carmel for winter break. The idea got his blood pumping: the two of them walking hand in hand on soft white sand against a purple sunset, the two of them naked and kissing in a bubbling Jacuzzi, the two of them rolling around on that enormous bed of fresh white linen; the embroidered pillows thrown on the floor, the air resplendent with the scent of lilacs, the murmurs of waves from outside the window coaxing them—moaning and groaning—on and on.

And, yeah, let's not forget, there's that Halloween party. Koala couldn't wait to see Cocky Bryan's face when he shows up at the wuss's frat house as Darma's guest. Isn't success the best revenge, after all, especially with a babe like Darma on his arm?

So it is then, the sun on his cheeks, his head full of possibilities, his body ripened for love, in that blur dream of optimism that Koala, ex-refugee, son of a dead Rade ethnic minority of Vietnam and a long, grieving mother, brother of a little boy buried at sea, highest scorer of the biochem midterm, and pre-med with upper-middle class American dream, kicks a three-legged mixed breed pug square in the ribs.

The flat-faced dog with droopy jowls has hopped out in front of him from behind a fire hydrant. Koala's foot makes contact with the animal before he sees it. The pug does not so much yelp as gives a resigned sigh, which sounded like a tiny whistle, then keels on its side. On its single hind leg it sits, stomach slouching, and stares up at his assailant with dull, blinking eyes. Koala watches as the dog licks its chops then slowly struggles back on its three legs and hops toward its owner, a gray-bearded man sitting next to the Bank of America ATM. A cardboard sign next to him reads: "Vietnam Vet. Hungry, please give."

When their eyes meet, the vet mutters: "Dang gook. You blind? Kicking a lame dawg?"

"What?" Koala's voice is choked from efforts to control his rage, which surges. "What just—what you called me, motherfucker?"

The hazy afternoon, which has existed until now in a vainglorious glow, begins to clarify itself: the pavement stops shimmering, is black-spotted with old chewing gum, the faces and bodies of the street vendors and pedestrians, even those of the young, take on a heavy definition. He feels the heat rising from the pavement. The world feels suddenly shallow and stunted.

"You're gonna get it," the vet says.

"What!"

"What's comin' to you."

"Fuck you." Koala drops his backpack, takes a fighting stance. A few passersby snicker. "Stand up, asshole! Right now. Right now, bitch! Stand up and get yours! Right now!" His stomach muscles tighten as heat rises to his face; his skin tingles.

"Watch it, you!" the vet says as he shrinks against the wall, arms raised to protect his head. But now he sees that Koala is not going to hit him, he rallies: in a slow, well-rehearsed gesture, the vet reaches into the side pocket of his tattered tweed jacket and produces a tarnished silver cigarette case.

"Oh, I see," Koala says with a smirk. "Mr. Hobo gonna smoke me to death."

The vet pops open the case. On a thin bed of yellow cotton sits a flat, shriveled mushroom, the color of night. "I killed myself . . ." the vet says, his voice as shaky as the hand that holds the case. "I killed half a dozen the likes of you. Here's what's left of one of them little gooks. So, don't fuck with me."

"What the . . ." Koala says in a whisper. His breath feels cold.

"Your ancestor's ear," the vet says. "Near Khe Sanh."

"Kay who?" Koala says. "Kay San what now?" The words sound vaguely familiar. He might have heard it mentioned once on PBS. His anger is replaced by a sense of threat, and under it, something obscure, a sensation that causes his heart to palpitate and slivers of ice to run in his blood. He leans down and squints for a better look. On the bed of yellowing cotton, the thing resembles, at first glance, a black chanterelle without a stem. Close up, however, he sees it for what it is—an ear, a shrunken left ear.

"Fuck," he says. The insides of his stomach churn. He can taste the bitter bile reaching the back of his throat. He feels heated. Restless. That thing belongs elsewhere—to the dark, to his father's deathbed whispers and his mother's murmurs, to ripened rice blades dripping with blood, to his father's world, scars and bombs and untold fairy tales, to chants and songs and incense smoke. To all the long dead. It does not belong here on Telegraph Avenue, amid bookstores and restaurants and cafes, with the sleek, colorful automobiles zooming by, all bathing under the sunlight.

"Fuck," he says again, and the anger dissipates toward curiosity. A sense of wonder overtakes him. Koala leans down as his arm moves of its own volition toward the thing.

The vet does not react. But his three-legged dog, as if on cue, jumps up and barks ferociously.

Koala steps back and stares. "Ahh," he says, drawing out each syllable, "Fuck. This. Shit!" He picks up his backpack and sprints.

Had he bothered to look across the street, he would have seen Bryan Cox leaning against a tree, eating a slice of Blondie's pizza, enthralled.

• • • •

What will forever etch itself into her memories is neither the terrible scuffles, nor Bryan Cox's cruel magic trick, but the surreal image on the ledge of the fraternity's second story window overlooking a garden that Hallow's Eve. A naked young man crouching there, his body scratched, face bruised, lips bleeding.

She'll see it so clearly in her mind's eye that in reveries, in dreams, she'll sometimes imagine it as painted—by a Girodet, or even a Caravaggio—and hung somewhere in a dusty hallway of her grandparents' brownstone villa on the outskirts of Florence. Always in the recalling there's a quality of light about him, a supernal glow from his olive skin as he perches there, framed by red velour curtains, its backdrop the succulent night.

She'll see again his left fist, clutching that grotesque thing like a precious gem. Behind her, a breathless, stunned audience—hushed spectators all to a daredevil act.

Koala, don't . . .

He turns, stares at her blankly, then back out the window where a tall oak and its many branches, like arms of a doting mother, beckons. If she could paint: a dash of red, a streak of gold-brown for lambent flesh, vague muscles unfold and flex; a blur toward darkness. A Francis Bacon figure; abstracted by yearning toward the dark.

She would call it *Night Flight*.

Earlier that evening: drinks and merriment.

The frat house on College Avenue exudes a playful kind of horror. It elicits smiles and giggles from those who walked and drove by. On the front lawn are several rows of tombstones and in the middle, a Gary Larson Holstein stands on her hind legs, wearing a pearl necklace, her alligator glasses askew. Her expression: that of a schoolmarm who has just opened her desk drawer to find a garden snake coiled about her ruler.

Koala and Darma arrive at the doorsteps, hand in hand, giggling. She wears a black dominatrix set—black vinyl halter bustier and mini skirt. In her hand, a riding crop. He wears a pair of low-waisted, Velcro black vinyl shorts that hug his ass snugly, and on his neck, a studded leather collar. They both shiver in the wind.

A tall musketeer opens the door and whistles lewdly at them both. Behind him, inside, monsters, fairies, demons, cowboys, Indians, crossdressers, kings and queens and superheroes whirl and gyrate. Music, sexy music, with a rhythm generated by a drum machine and a continuous, repeating bass line, like invisible hands, pulls them toward the dancing mass. He lifts her up, howls, and together they spin toward the dance floor.

How can such a festive night end so disastrously?

• • • •

I'll send you home. Honest. My money is right here, in that ATM behind you.

Twin Falls. It's really far. I've been trying, man . . .

So—say $250 dollars on Greyhound will get you to TF?

What about Ray?

Ray who?

Ray, my dawg.

Take him with you. I'll throw in another twenty.

Ain't leaving without Ray. Named him after my best bud. Sniper got him.

No reason why you should. The way he looks, Ray ain't walking there on his own. Twin Falls's nice?

Beautiful, how I remember it.

So, we got a deal? What'd you say, hero?

• • • •

The library on the second floor of the fraternity mansion is something of an architectural treasure. Designed in Greek Revival style, its two tall, stately windows look out to a walled garden below. Large antique writing desks with their clawed legs flank three walls. On built-in shelves in two opposite walls are first editions in vellum and rare books bound in calf-gilt, or still in their original dust jackets. The collection is not to be read so much as admired, a pantheon of Western geniuses to inspire one and all.

Walking through the ionic columns at the square opening, Koala is assaulted with a sense of high-style splendor and a faint but pervasive smell of old leather. Under his feet, the Oriental rug in a passion fruit and roses motif is so plush that he feels as if the earth itself is pushing up from beneath the foundation of the house to challenge the faux Raphael painted ceiling depicting, as Darma points out to him, the scene of "School of Athens" framed by elaborate cove molding above.

In its center, amidst the circling crowd, a wizard commands attention. A few acts have been performed by the frat boys—including a vampire quartet crooning "Blue Moon" and a clown juggling bowling balls—but the wizard commands attention when lights dim and Steppenwolf's "Magic Carpet Ride" echoes from the stereo.

A gesture of the wizard's arm and a dove flies out from seemingly nowhere. It flaps frantically over the gawking crowd before heading out the open window and into the night.

Amidst applause the wizard brushes a tiny feather off his sleeve. Peter Pan, his assistant, brings out a red balloon and a few thin and long needles. A girl with cat whiskers and a pink nose next to Koala sucks in her breath loudly as the wizard slowly pushes one needle after another through the fleshy balloon and it stays inflated. An Elvis standing next to Koala makes a lewd joke but is quickly hushed. The wizard pulls the needle out slowly, one by one, and the balloon remains unharmed.

"Hold your applause," says the wizard as the crowd cheers. "And watch this!" He tosses the balloon up in the air. It comes down between his hands—and pops into a puff of smoke from which another flapping dove emerges. He throws it up in the air, and it flies in several circles before finding its escape route out one of the two windows.

It is suddenly very hot in the library. Koala feels dizzy, dehydrated. He plucks at his leather collar. He chastises himself for doing one too many tequila shots with the Black cowboy downstairs during the dancing. Now he desperately wants water. He looks for Darma but cannot find her.

He is about to leave when Peter Pan brings out an easel with a painting hidden under a cloth. "Up till now, it was but child's play," the wizard's voice rings out, "but what I am about to do next is no trick, dames and knights, spirits and beasts. No. 'Tis true magic."

"Observe," he says and nods to Peter Pan, who promptly removes the cloth above the easel. A hushed murmur rises from the crowd. On the canvas, a grim, bearded face with haunted eyes peers out to the audience from a half-turned angle. Where the man's ear should be, a space is left unpainted.

"You all know who this great artist is, I presume?" the wizard says. "Know what the man did to himself in that little room of his in Arles?" There are a few nervous chuckles in the library. The lights dim further, and after a surge of disrespectful giggling and jeers, silence falls. "My arcane powers will render, shall we say, the artist whole again."

How Bryan Cox manages it, Koala doesn't know. He knows what is coming but doesn't know how. He wants to leave. He tries, but his feet stay rooted. His stomach churns. Nausea rises in the form of acid that burns the back of his throat. He keeps his eyes shut. Even before the incantation, he already sees it on the easel, filling that blank space. It doesn't belong there. It belongs at the bottom of the sea. Buried under sand and rubble. Floating down rivers, in the rain. To bodies rotting to the bone, back into mud.

Memories of another world surge from deep within him as the wizard chants his incantation. A small explosion resounds, like that of the flash bulb going off from an old press camera.

Ooh, says the crowd.

"What is that thing?" a pixie next to him asks.

"Oh shit," someone else says. "I think it's for real. Dude, that's fucked up. Bryan's crazy!" There is nervous laughter.

Koala still keeps his eyes closed. He cannot bear to look. He hears snippets of the wizard's speech and triumph in his voice.

A real ear . . .

distant past . . .

forgotten corner . . .

a little room, halfway around the world . . . on this portrait . . . come close and inspect, boys.

It's real, folks. Touch it if you . . .

He steels himself before opening his eyes. On the canvas, the vet's trophy is now attached to where the blank space had been—all the while, Van Gogh's piercing blue eyes continue to stare accusingly at him.

Then another face appears in front him. Behind its fake beard, which glitters with little stars and a crescent moon, it seems to be smirking.

"Well, slave, what bethink thee of my charms?"

• • • •

If his mind still functioned normally, Koala wouldn't be able to explain it. Some other self has taken over, a dark, powerful rage. This then, his answer to the wizard: a swift punch to the guts, then quickly, a shove to the Roman sentry who is leaning close to inspect the ear.

Rips it off, knocking over the canvas.

A vampire grabs Koala's shoulder and gets elbowed in the face and screams, clutching his mouth.

The sentry recovers and punches Koala in the chest. Koala's hand chops the sentry's temple, and his plastic helmet flies off, and the boy makes a muffled sound as he goes down on his knees.

"Guys! Guys!" Bryan Cox manages while hugging his stomach. "Oh my god, stop!"

Koala hears Darma screeching. She's on the back of a werewolf who was about to hit him with a chair but whose attention now is fully diverted to getting the red-haired dominatrix off his hairy back.

The vampire, still on his knees, suddenly lunges at Koala's legs, and another vampire grabs his arms. Someone turns off the light, scuffles and screams follow, and when the lights are restored, Koala has lost his shoes and shorts and is bleeding from the lips, his back against the bookshelves and both vampires are on the ground.

"Fucker! Give back Bryan's ear," yells an angry Peter Pan who rushes Koala. But before he reaches him, Koala's leg flies out in a perfect sidekick to the boy's solar plexus and Peter Pan grunts and doubles over.

"Fuck! Tony's hurt, bad," someone says, and before others can attack him, Koala reacts instinctively. He turns, and with his one free hand, starts to throw books from the shelves indiscriminately at everyone nearby.

Roget's Thesaurus, the unabridged edition, hits the male Cinderella smack in the nose and causes his wig to fly. Dostoevsky's *Brothers Karamazov*, hardcover, flies at the wizard's face, and he ducks, and it knocks his hat off instead. To the clown's nose goes the spine of William James's *The Varieties of Religious Experience*, while *Art and Illusion* by Ernst H. Gombrich flies to the Green Lantern, who barely has time to raise his arms to block it. *A Vision* by W. B. Yeats slips from his grip, so Koala grabs Jean-Jacques Rousseau's *Confessions* and is about to throw it when a screaming scarecrow appears with a baseball bat and swings. He jumps. The bat slams into a bookshelf behind him.

The Black cowboy who had downed tequila shots with Koala earlier downstairs steps in behind the scarecrow and holds him in a half nelson until he drops the bat.

"Stop, guys, all of you, stop it." He hears Bryan's trembling voice. "I didn't want this."

And a Jolly Green Giant stands between the two vampire boys and Koala, his arms raised. "Yeah, hold on, y'all," he says in a loud, throaty voice, "before you destroy the library."

"Yeah," agrees the Black cowboy, and with authority, taking his fake shiny gun out and aiming it at the painted ceiling, "y'all just COOL it right now!"

Someone snickers.

Koala takes advantage of the moment, climbs onto the windowsill. Heads turn.

The moon shines bright outside. And below, the garden glistens under its pale light. The oak beckons. He takes a breath—

Koala, don't.

—and leaps.

• • • •

How long does it take to enter the night?

A second. All one's born days.

Traveling through the cool air, something unravels within him. All at once, he is preternaturally thrilled and terrified.

Koala manages to grab hold of a lower branch with one hand, in the other, he clutches the ear. His chest makes an impact with the lower branch, and he loses his grip. And falls. He hears it before he feels it—the crunch in his right knee at a bad angle—and screams as he crumbles-tumbles to the ground.

Lying there on his back among the unkempt grass, he finds himself a recipient of a myriad of strange senses. Shooting pains. The incredibly sweet smell of wet earth and grass of jasmine and fresh herbs, redolent in the breeze: he hears the chirping of a cricket in the next garden; iridescent patterns streak and tread like a net in the night sky— they connect everything to everything else—a world, a dancing, shimmering spider web.

"Let's get him," yells someone from above.

"Oh, no you don't," yells Darma. There is more scuffling above in the library, some screeching.

Koala struggles to stand on his one good leg, dragging himself toward the tree, and leans his back against its trunk, panting.

He hears footsteps. Three shadows emerge from the house. Now he's surrounded by a male Cinderella, a Roman sentry, and a vampire. The male princess, with his tiara askew on his wig, looks especially ridiculous and Koala laughs.

"Give us back Bryan's ear," Cinderella announces, his nose still bleeding, his face scowled and menacing. "Then get on your knees, motherfucker, and beg us to spare you."

"This?" Koala manages a smirk as he unclenches his left fist. There on his palm lies the winkled little thing like a little raft on the sea.

"Why the fuck did you take Bryan's ear anyway?" the vampire next to the male Cinderella asks.

No. Not Bryan's ear. Someone else's.

From some distant garden, a dog starts barking.

Koala looks up again at the three boys. He suddenly sees the flash of that knife; the vet as a young man. The blood splattered on the muddy ground.

"No," he manages. "It's mine."

Even as part of him contemplates a strategy to save himself from a beating, Koala's hand is obeying some other instinct: he sees himself smiling to his enemies with bloody lips, sees his arm raised as if to offer the thing that could save him. But as if willed by another's volition, he delivers it toward his open mouth.

Koala tastes leather and his own blood.

"Fuckin' gross!" says the vampire, stepping backward.

Koala looks up defiantly at his assailants.

"Fucking cannibal!" The Roman sentry turns away.

The mustached princess says nothing. Before he acts, however, Bryan Cox rushes up from behind and delivers a kick to Koala's left side.

He feels something crack as he rolls into a fetal position.

He is barely aware of Darma's voice ringing out above him. "Get away from him, fucking asshole," she shrieks. He hears the whoosh of her riding crop hitting flesh repeatedly and Bryan screaming in pain. "Get away from him, you butt wipes."

"Yeah, guys, forget it," a young woman echoes from the library's window. "Tony's okay. He's okay. Bryan? Please? The cops are coming!"

Koala hears retreating footsteps. He feels a silky thigh slipping under his head and a few drops of rain on his face. Or are they tears? A finger wipes the blood from his lips.

"Damn it, Koala. You have a lot of explaining to do. You son of a bitch!"

He knows it's there, wracking with pain, but he can't feel his body. He gazes at her, tries to smile, and fails. With great effort, he takes the ear out of his mouth, to show her his triumph. The ear feels viscous now, bathing in blood and saliva. It feels warm in his trembling hand when he spits back out.

"Crazy fuck," she whispers, then sniffles.

Another presence in the garden. The buzz and crackle of a walkie-talkie. He hears some vague conversation above him as he slowly fades. "Son, I need you stay awake," a mature man's voice says to him. "What's your name, son?" He sees a shadow above him. Then a bright light goes searing now into his bruised eyes. He feels blunt fingers pulling open his eyelids. Koala mumbles: "Koa . . ." but changes his mind. "Bang. Bang . . ." he manages in a whisper, "Cao Y Le Bang."

"What's the date today, son? Do you know today's date?"

He shakes his head lightly. He wants to confess to the shadow above him that he cheated on Jenkins's test. He wants to profess his love to Darma, that he doesn't think his sadness will ever go away no matter what he does. But he can no longer speak.

His attention is elsewhere. To the garden, which has grown brighter and glowing, its leaves and trees all luminesce, and in the air, silvery strands are wavering. They coil into a luminous serpent.

He hears voices.

Y Bang! Y Bang!

You're gonna get it!

DNA in one human body unraveled would reach the moon and back 8,000 times . . .

The iridescent strands turn now into his father's coffin being lowered into the ground. They weave into the secondhand gray blazer his younger self wore as he stood awkwardly next to his weeping mother. They turned into waves on an open sea.

His body convulses. He can barely breathe. He hears his own wheezing. His lungs on fire.

The wind blows stronger now, and the grass and leaves waver. It caresses his wounds, entering his blood.

Darma's voice is hysterical.

"Koala, stay with me. Ambulance's coming! Can you hear it? Shit! Koala, please! Ambulance's coming!"

Koala wants to tell her that he is okay, but he can no longer remember the words. The sounds of something wailing, the oak branches intermittently flash like lightning in red, in silver. The shrieking grows louder, and nearer, like a child being born somewhere nearby and it is howling in the middle of an unforgiving tempest.

October Laments

LH posted a photo and a note.

Nov. 01 at 1:47 a.m.

You will not come back in my dreams, I know, but if you can, please let her see you again? Because if 25 years of sharing life is not enough for me, then for the baby 14 years, how—how? How is this enough? So little! So please!

Photo: The Golden Gate Bridge in the distance as viewed from her living room window, the fog rolling in, barely visible but for one of its two towers. The Pacific, partially glimpsed, is gray and somber.

LH shared a memory.

Oct. 30 at 11:21 p.m.

This day, that year 2012! Halloween in our neighborhood! Look, look at the dancing Harlequins. Look! Look!

Photo: Adults dressed up in costumes going trick-or-treating. In the center: two harlequins in black-and-white checkered shirts with maroon satin sleeves, the really tall one is wearing a skull mask. He's holding a silvery pinwheel toy, and it is spinning in a blur. He's Big Man. And Big Man is looking admiringly at LH. She, with a half domino mask and in a very short skirt and mismatched knee stockings, is holding a silver gun with a gold flag. The flag, of course, says "Bang!" But if there's any reference to Nabokov's novel exploring polygamy, it's not self-evident. This is true love.

LH wrote a comment, marking herself as sad.

Oct. 30 at 11:02 p.m.

What if you could make it to the 77th? Big Man, the menu I cook tonight might be long, and we could have the biggest party ever! The big double seven in life! Oh! Time machine! Why are you driving only one direction?!!!

LH shared a comment without photo.

Oct. 30 at 2:12 p.m.

In memoriam of the phone call you made in the last century from San Francisco to Saigon in the year no. 8 of our relationship! You said: "You know what? I was driving on the highway, then I thought 'hell, let's do it!' And I turned to the jewelry store. There I found the ring fit me well, exactly the way I like! How about that!"

The guy who swore to be single forever met a career woman in Saigon. He started to wonder at the year no. 5 how she can walk away after saying goodbye in the airport on trip after trip around the world with him. She never had the answer for any of his suggestions about "leaving everything in Saigon to just be with me in San Francisco!"

He kept counting the years, she kept going back to her hometown . . .

He ended the call by saying "I dream to have a wedding one time in my life! With you, my darling! Could you meet me in Hong Kong in March?"

After some silence, this Saigon Businesswoman said: "Ok! Sure!" And she bought her ticket. And voilà!

LH posted a photo.
Oct. 29 at 8:02 p.m.
Offering to the Big Man
Who traveled, who loved, who admired all the cultures of humankind!
Fresh hibiscus!
Happy Chhath Puja!

Photo: A shrub of big, bloodred hibiscus draping over a thin and tall blue crystal vase on a wooden table. Behind the table is a cabinet on which two white candles are burning. A dozen persimmons form a pyramid on a porcelain plate between them, a vision of plenty. Behind the persimmons sits a framed black-and-white photo of Big Man, who smiles warmly to the world.

LH posted a video.
Oct. 29 at 3:44 p.m.
Here is Big Man on Aztec antiquities 4 years ago. They know time. They plant. They harvest. They sacrifice around the clock. Hahaha!

At Yerba Buena center, here he is, ladies and gentlemen, for your pleasure!

Video: Big Man in a beige suit giving a lecture. On the screen behind him, an image of an Aztec Calendrical Wheel. "The calendar, through the use of the location of the stars, sun, and moon, was an instrument to calculate planting, feasting, and harvesting, and also trading times," he said in a booming voice. "The Aztec cycle lasted fifty-two years. When the calendar ended, the Aztecs did what is called a New Fire Ceremony. During this ceremony, the Aztecs prayed for the sun to rise again, and when it did, made sacrifices in gratitude to the gods for another fifty-two-year cycle."

Below the video, LH wrote a comment at 8:52 p.m.
We only got 25 years, baby!!
So I sacrifice: half my heart, half my soul.

LH shared a memory.
    Oct. 29 at 4:43 a.m.
This day, last year! I found this note you left on your desk. It was written: "The verb to die can also mean to marry the earth in Nahuatl!"
I wish that you will be happy with this new marriage . . . this time, exactly 1 year. As you decided!

Photo: Handwritten note on an old writing desk. The lighting is too dim, the image slightly out of focus. But we see a small replica of an Aztec Calendrical Wheel partially captured next to it.

LH shared a memory.
    Oct. 28 at 2:02 a.m.
This day, three years ago, this note! Time Machine, time, time, time machine!

Photo: A note. The handwriting is that of Big Man. It has her name written out in Vietnamese. "Her name means Perfume of the Orchid. Idea: Maybe a locket for her 45th? Maybe a bottle of Perfume in the shape of an orchid? Maybe dinner at a 3 Michelin Star restaurant (stars look like orchids, no? Maybe I'm pushing it.)"

LH posted a photo.
    Oct. 27 at 11:11 p.m.
Following Paul Newman, who left a famous Rolex, Big Man also left one. He bought this the year he went to Vietnam to work for USAID during VN War 1967, the year I was born.

The Rolex is for the kid, his beloved baby. One day, she will wear it during her diving trips along with Big Man's adopted whale, also named after Big Man . . . She will whisper to giant whale's ears, "Dad loved you as much as I do"!

Photo: A 1967 Rolex, known as the Sea-Dweller. It's waterproof up to 610 meters. Perfect for professional drivers. It sits inside the original green Rolex box. A thing of beauty. The time, 11:11:23.

LH shared a memory.
    Oct. 27 at 11:16 p.m.
    I had 24 hours to go through the countdown! I did feel how a hand could go from warm to cold. It was the longest quiet moment between us after 25 years. I did think "I have to accept this because that's what you wish for!" If I did let you do all what you want in the life we shared, I should respect your decision how your life should end! Why suffer unnecessarily?
    But I see your Rolex on this nightstand. I see it tick-ticking. I keep thinking: it keeps going, why not your heart?

Two photos: Image of Big Man in a hospital bed, eyes closed, tubes through his nose, an IV unit attached to his arm. A doctor by his bedside, looking somber. Another image of Big Man's Rolex on the hospital nightstand. Too blurry for us to tell the time.

LH shared a photo.
    Oct. 27 at 5:20 p.m.
    Cúng 2018.
    Offerings for the Big Man!
    Khổ qua trắng hầm a.k.a. white bitter gourd filling with ground pork mushroom and vermicelli in the broth.
    Caramélises pork with fish sauce.

Chicken porridge.
Banana flower salad with chicken.
Steamed rice.
Sweet corn pudding with coconut cream and roasted sesame.
Grapes on the vine, fruit of the season.
Fresh white orchid.
Bon appetit!

Photo: Round silver tray with many small dishes assembled as if petals to a sunflower. Around the tray are jasmine branches spread out like a diadem, the tray with its many offerings serving as the crown jewel. Slightly out of frame, north of this tray, is a small bowl of rice with three joss sticks burning, smoke wafting in the air.

LH is tagged in a photo by her daughter on her page.
    Oct. 26 at 11:35 p.m.
    "Mama is cooking again. I am getting so fat just watching," her daughter wrote. "Does she even sleep?"

Photo: LH is standing in the tiny kitchen, smiling to the camera. It is full of pots and pans and dishes. The Golden Gate barely visible behind her out the window.

At 11:44 p.m., LH added a comment below that photo.

I cook what I want to invite you to taste, Big Man. I cook to highlight the 25 years of happiness we had. Our baby gained weight because she ate your portion, hahahha!

Hope that you are satisfied with the offering tonight! From my kitchen to you! With all my heart!

LH shared a video.

    Oct. 26 at 11:20 p.m.

    Big Man.

I am watching *Out of Africa* again for the *n*th time, listening to the melody of the soundtrack and remembering how mature we were! In love! Because we did move beyond all of the boundaries of life and reached the end of a story!

Video: Scene where Meryl Streep gets her hair shampooed by Robert Redford under blue sky. He pours water over her hair. She, her eyes closed, is in ecstasy.

LH shared a video.

    Oct. 26 at 10:23 p.m.

Lying on the bedsheet made of linen becomes a heavenly time for a dream every night!!! The more I wash, the cooler it is. Miss you! Look at us now. You who now married Nahuatl! Me who is trying to divorce Time Machine! Hahaha!

Video: A well-made bed. She is not lying in it. The camera pans back and forth between two pillows, but the camera is shaking and the scene out of focus.

LH shared a memory.

    Oct. 25 at 3:42 a.m.

    Dear Big Man!

Three more days—almost one year already since you married the earth. I know it's countdown time then! I count down again now. I do understand we cannot go against the Time Machine. It takes you forward. It won't drive anybody back. I know.

But how to accept this fact? I still wish it could be as different as I would like it to be!

Not for you, not for me, but for our baby!

Miss you, miss, miss, miss you dearly!!!

Photo: Big Man, still healthy, in fact, robust, and LH who is holding their daughter at two, all laughing to the camera.

LH shared a memory.

Oct. 25 at 1:22 a.m.

Big Man,

You are gone but your gift for me is still here!

Thanks a lot! For always saying "Why not?" to me and encouraging me to overcome my failures to reach the level I dreamed about! So I came to America. To You.

If there is a next lifetime, you know well, I have the same dream of the same life we shared together! I'll drive this time machine to the starting point. Haha.

Video: Big Man in the garden at Stanford's hospital in his hospital gown. The sun is shining. He is squinting at the camera and in a warm, if hoarse, voice, recites Hardy's "I Look into My Glass."

"I look into my glass,
And view my wasting skin,
And say, 'Would God it came to pass
My heart had shrunk as thin!'"

Here, Big Man pauses, becomes distracted by the sunlight. At length, he continues:

"For then I, undistrest
By hearts grown cold to me . . ."

He stops again to breathe. His breath is labored.

After a while, Big Man gathers himself and continues . . .

"Could lonely wait my endless rest
With equanimity.

But Time, to make me grieve,
   Part steals, lets part abide;
   And shakes this fragile frame at eve
   With throbbings of noontide."

"Beautiful, baby," LH is heard whispering behind her camera. "Beautiful."

LH is tagged by her daughter in a short video.
   Oct. 22 at 8:22 p.m.

Video: She's standing in the kitchen over a steaming pot of soup, ladle in hand. She is smiling to the camera.

"What this tiktac tiktac thing? I should get this? Like a clock? Like a time machine?" she asked.

We hear her daughter giggling behind the camera: "No, Mom, it's TikTok, and please, don't even think about it."

Then we hear the daughter mumble: "Gawd, Mom on TikTok, that's like uhm End of days."

LH shared a photo.
   Oct. 22 at 4:42 p.m.
   Early offering To the Big Man
   Who loved all the cultures of humankind!
   Fresh peonies from Israel!

Photo: Three big, bloodred peonies in a blue vase on a table. Behind the table is a cabinet from which black-and-white photos of the dead stare out

at the world of the living. Two white candles stand tall, burning. A dozen
persimmons sit between them.

LH wrote a poem.
  Oct. 23 at 3:40 a.m.
  Poem for Big Man (don't laugh at my English, OK)

  You OK, Moon?
  Night, are you happy?
  Sun will rise in an hour
  Night you will be gone, gone for a while
  Moon, Sun, Night, Day oh I
  will long for the infinity of time
  Fog horns cry and cry
  Clouds and fog cover the sky
  How do people understand my smile?
  Love you, I do, from Neptune to Venus, thrice!

LH shared a photo.
  Oct. 24 at 9:57 p.m.
  Cooking of the day!
  Offering for the Big Man!
  Chè bắp nước cốt dừa lá dứa a.k.a. corn pudding with coconut cream
and pandan leaves.
  In memoriam of the love you had for Hội An! The only place in
Vietnam where you dreamed of building up a Maritime Museum
to show evidence of the maritime history of the Vietnamese Coast
throughout humankind civilization. It will be the strongest manifesto
of the ownership of all that belongs to Vietnam in a thousand years.
  The dream you had for Vietnam was with you till the last day!
  Here it is. The dessert of the land and the people you loved!!!

Photo: A small blue bowl of corn pudding in coconut cream nestles inside an intricate white bowl shaped like a giant snowflake.

LH shared a memory.
Oct. 24 at 7:21 a.m.
The happiness before! Miss the trip where we went to Cuba so much! It was the last time you had cigar and rum, and baby and I jumped up and down on the sand, run to the ocean! But the trip back to Galapagos to visit your adopted whale not to be! When will it be? Little Big Man, you are an orphan now, baby. Your godfather is traveling now in Underworld!

Photo: Mother and daughter jumping up above a sandy beach, the sea glistening like gold behind them. Assumedly, Big Man took this photograph.

LH shared another poem and photo.
Oct. 23 at 11:42 p.m.

Hoa rơi sao quá nhẹ nhàng
Thời gian ngưng đọng đợi . . . ngàn hạc bay!!!

(Author's translation:
Petals fall ever so gently
Time stands so still . . .
Waiting for a thousand cranes to take flight)

Photo: The top shelf of an old dark wood cabinet on top of which various photos of the family are on display, along with a singular white orchid plant whose flowers are slightly wilted. Well-folded white crane origamis are scattered everywhere on the shelf, amidst the photos, like fallen petals.

LH shared a video.
Oct. 23 at 8:20 p.m.
This time, two years ago. Big Man your 76th.

Video: Her husband is singing "Happy Birthday" with their young daughter next to him, his arm protective over her shoulders. The girl is all smiles and seems slightly embarrassed. There is laughter in the background as well. Big Man's voice is baritone, warm. Father and daughter rock back and forth in sync, as if they are on a boat. "To life!" he says while staring straight into the camera with a shot glass in hand. "And also single malt whiskey!" LH is heard laughing uncontrollably behind the camera.

LH shared a photo.
Oct. 22 at 11:22 p.m.
The way you looked at me! As happy as the Spring comes early!

Photo: Big Man healthy and happy, standing tall and in a tuxedo. He is staring toward his bride wearing a simple white wedding dress, and he is grinning ear to ear. Assumedly in the early years. His hair is still blond. He looks very young and vigorous for a man in his mid-sixties, a straight back, muscular arms.

LH shared a photo.
Oct. 22 at 10:11 p.m.
What if I said no? What if I said, "No, don't get that ring." What if I said, "We date OK. Marriage not ok?" Would I be happy now in Saigon? Still running my art gallery back there? Or sad in Saigon, thinking of what I could have had in San Francisco?

Photo: A very young LH in her art gallery where she eventually met Big

Man. She's smiling widely to the camera behind her trademark big black rim glasses. She's young and thin, and her smile is untroubled.
LH shared a video as filmed by her daughter.
  Oct. 14, 2017 at 2:43 p.m.

Video: "Everyone say hello to Big Man." LH herself is seen FaceTiming with a group of friends. Big Man is seen over her shoulders looking at the screen. "He is not well. He loves your hellos."
  A chorus of people can be heard through her phone's speaker mode.
  "Hi, Big Man, big hug."
  "Happy birthday," someone else yelled.
  "We love you, G . . ." a man yells. Others follow.

Big Man seems very frail in the video. He tries to raise his arm, but it barely lifts over his stomach, restrained by IV tubes and gravity.
  "LH, please kiss him for me," another woman is heard on the phone yelling. "Sending all my love."
  Big Man seems beyond exhausted. He tries to speak, but he has no voice. But it's typical of him, he smiles, his eyes still carry that boyish expression, which endears him to one and all.

Nov. 15, 2020 at 5:19 a.m.
  Below the above video, LH added a livestream video.

Video: LH is behind the camera as it is showing an empty desk. We hear her voice. "Time Machine . . . you work better than any Swiss watch but only forward . . . You send us so far to the future now . . . Even when we get daylight savings time, you still beat us. Hahaha! I'm trying to go back to where happiness is. I scroll down and down till when Big Man is alive. I post and I post like this mad woman. But it is so hard. You win Time Machine. Okay. You win. Okay. We drive forward."

The camera pans slowly out to the window: we can barely make out the

Golden Gate Bridge hidden behind the fog. It is almost dawn. A ray of sunlight pierces upward to simmer the pinkish sky.

If you listen very carefully, you can hear the widow sniffing quietly as the foghorn intermittently blows its singular note.

A Good Broth Takes Its Time

A bright Saigon morning in March. At Mrs. Tran's restaurant on Pasteur Street, bad news came blaring on the radio. Da Nang was under attack. Two Russian MIGs had flown all the way from Hanoi to the central highlands without ARVN resistance. Bombarded by VC mortar, the city was veiled in black smoke.

Everyone—customers, waiters, a dozen passersby, even Mrs. Tran's mangy, flea-bitten German shepherd—all held their breath and listened. The plump and sturdy matron stayed too, her cleaver on the large chopping block where she'd been slicing beef tripe. With eyes closed, she listened. Her husband, a captain in the Marines, was stationed north of Da Nang. Since mid-February, she had no news of him.

Customers broke out in gossip when the special news report ended, some openly wept over their uneaten soup, others, their faces ashen, pushed out their chairs, stood up, and left without paying. Mrs. Tran didn't care. She began to remove her jade bracelet, gold Buddha necklace, and two ruby earrings, then wrapped them in a white handkerchief. She handed the tiny bundle to her daughter, Nga, the dreamy-eyed teenager who was busy staring at the bright street outside, where flame trees bloomed red and orange, and where people rushed here and there in a state of panic.

"Stop daydreaming, my child," Mrs. Tran scolded. "Put this away and write this down. Get pen and paper. You should have memorized it by now, the way you devour poetry, but I know you haven't. And may Lady Buddha Quan Yin protect us all."

Allow the oxtail and marrow bones to unleash their flavor, and the star anise and cloves to permeate thoroughly, making it a worthy base for the delicate rice noodles, which are, as you know, freshly cooked for each bowl.

In 1967, in the middle of the monsoon season, fifty South Vietnamese soldiers with Northern accents and ancestry, in a program concocted by the CIA, parachuted back into northern territories to act as spies. Of the fifty, Mr. Chi Nguyen was the only one who managed to elude capture and blend in with the general populace.

Now in Sacramento, California, a wizened old man with a toothless grin and a throaty voice, Mr. Nguyen told his story to a pot-bellied reporter from the *Sacramento Bee*. Having infiltrated Hanoi, he ordered pho in a well-known restaurant near Hoan Kiem Lake. In the middle of eating his soup, he spotted Vu, his best friend and comrade in espionage, sitting at another table. They made eye contact but did not dare talk. Mr. Nguyen desperately wanted to warn Vu to stop slurping so loudly, as he was attracting attention. But before he could gesture or say a word, Vu already made a second mistake, which proved fatal: he ordered a second bowl.

Customers and waiters gasped. Heads turned. For it was a time of rationing and self-sacrifice, a time of anti-bourgeois behaviors, and no one, not even Uncle Ho himself, ever ordered a second bowl. Eat a second bowl and you'd have committed an anti-revolutionary act. Eat too much and you'd have shown your true bourgeois colors. Eat more than your share and you'd never survive the communist paradise.

Like the others from the group, Vu was promptly arrested, tortured, then, four months later, executed on espionage charges. Mr. Nguyen himself survived by sheer luck: he had a small stomach and, besides, had never forgotten the unforgiving nature of the North.

After the war ended, he left the country on a boat with his wife and children. The wife, a peasant, did not know that he was a spy for the South until they reached the United States. The children, too busy becoming Americans, didn't care. But it was not his story of espionage that Mr. Nguyen recalled now with fondness. It was his first bowl of soup in Hanoi. "You know what," he said to the reporter in a voice now tinged with longing. "It was the best bowl of pho I ever had. Simple, but delicious. No garnish, just a squeeze of lime on a few pieces of raw beef the size of your fingernail, and the broth—oh la la, it smelled distinctly of star anise and charred onion."

"I was hungry with my eyes and nose, even if my stomach couldn't hold," said Mr. Nguyen. "If I could have eaten like Vu, poor bastard, I probably would have, at the risk of death and destruction, ordered another bowl." Then, at the thought of his own death and destruction, the old man fell into a laughing fit that almost killed him, and his eyes, tearing, disappeared under wrinkling epicanthic folds.

Mr. Nguyen grew three kinds of basil in his garden in Sacramento, plus a few other herbs, like Vietnamese coriander, lemongrass, mint, and many star anise bushes and some parsnip. "So where is home now for you, Mr. Nguyen?" asked the *Bee* reporter.

Home, he said, is his pungent garden, home is the hot summer breeze in which herbal aromas waft and fold. Home is what you run away from in your youth, only to be trapped again in longing for it in your old age. Faraway restaurants are known to order his anise and coriander. "Smell this," he said, as he mashed a dark green basil leaf between his tobacco-stained fingers and held its fragrant juice against the reporter's nose. "Smell good, yes, yes? This smell, it makes me remember, it takes me all the way back."

To make pho, be of many minds. The side dishes alone can distract you from the main broth. The broth demands constant care, for without it, my dear, you have nothing.

Late afternoon of the last day of April in 1975, the sun burned like a piece of coal overhead, an eerie silence reigned over the entire city, and Communist tanks crashed through the gilded gates of an empty Independence Palace. Inside, a fat president named Big Minh, who had been president for a day, sat waiting to surrender. The city had fallen, and young VCs sat on rusty, mud-caked trucks and rusty tanks with looks of awe and bewilderment on their sunburnt faces. Saigon was beautiful, rich beyond their imagination, not the poor, wretched place suffering under imperial powers their leaders had filled their heads with all those years in the jungle. Already, some began to ponder that question that is still argued to this day: who's liberating whom?

From behind curtains and over red and purple bougainvillea-veiled walls, and hidden behind tamarind and flame trees, well-fed, discreet Saigonese stole glimpses at their emaciated conquerors, while a few of their rowdier children climbed the walls and, thinking it was yet another military parade, hollered and waved.

At the dock, it was another story. Thousands had gathered and were jostling each other onto the planks of waiting ships. Nga herself boarded a crowded boat with her younger brother. Their aunt was with them. Nga's mother had accompanied the three to the dock but decided to stay and wait for news of her husband. Her aged parents, besides, needed her back in Quang Ngai province, if they'd survived. But even if they hadn't, she needed to fulfill her filial duties and bury them properly. With hoarse, weeping voices, Nga, her little brother, and their young aunt all begged Mrs. Tran to come along—"Please, sister, I beg you, think of the children!"; "Oh mother, how can you possibly not come?"; "Ma, I'm so scared!" But Mrs. Tran was adamant. "Go! Go with my blessing. And you, take care of my children like your own," she ordered her younger sister, and hastily stuffed all the gold and dollars she had traded earlier that morning into her sister's and daughter's outreached hands. She imagined herself giving away the dowry at her daughter's wedding, which she, in a flash of prescience, saw as taking place on a kept lawn and beside a lake dotted with sailboats. She even saw the groom's face, a smiling, blue-eyed stranger who was now lifting her daughter's pearl-studded veil to kiss her.

The ship engine rumbled, the smell of diesel assaulted the air, Mrs. Tran's children called out desperately for their mother, but she kept walking. She willed herself not to look back, not even once. On the streets and sidewalks near the dock, motorbikes and cars and army jeeps and suitcases and clothes were left abandoned. And in the air, Vietnamese dong—green, red, and orange—fluttered like butterflies.

The colorful South Vietnamese currency had lost all its value that morning and was now worth only as much as the paper mock-offerings one burned for the dead. However, the street urchins did not know this. A band of them, wearing new clothes that were too big for them, were amassing the notes they had coveted for so long, singing gleefully their prophetic ditty of what was to come.

In the dying light of April, Mrs. Tran mumbled her Buddhist prayers while clutching her rosary made from seeds of a Bodhi tree, which were shiny from years of use. She kept on walking. Behind her, one ship after another left the harbor.

A bowl of pho with marrow served on the side is treasure. A dish of oxtail bone to accompany it, sprinkled with green onion, black pepper and freshly chopped chili, is love.

A windy autumn morning in the mid-1960s, the sky a benevolent blue, the war undecided, a handsome young man named Quang set sail. Long before leaving was thought possible, before "*vượt biên*"—to cross the border—was to become a household word, Quang alone had already seen the seven seas. A genius with pipes and propellers, a doctor of ailing engines, he could hear their unquiet murmurs and name their ailments without fail. He would then set out to fix them and made himself indispensable to the Golden Seahorse shipping line from Hong Kong, who paid a small fortune to the foreign department in Saigon to purchase his exit visa and, in doing so, gave him the world.

The night before he left, his mother, pricking her thigh with a small hairpin under the table so that she wouldn't have to pay attention to the real pain of losing her only son, said in a stern voice: "Go! Please go! I'd rather have you alive in Morocco than coming back to me in a body bag from the DMZ. Go! Save yourself. And listen to me, unless there is real peace, don't you dare come back."

So, there was a war, and he was sailing far away from it. There was a war, and he didn't sleep well in any port or on any ocean. The Tet offensive, and he was in Madagascar. His mother's death, and he wept all the way to Iceland. His best friend mortally wounded in An Loc, and he watched a gorgeous sunset from Sydney with a Chivas Regal bottle as his companion.

When the war ended and the South lost, he couldn't come home. He kept his promise to his mother and kept going, though Quang kept dreaming of his homeland and everyone he knew there. His yearning over time made him at once handsome yet impossibly aloof. He had no friends, and his lovers were fleeting and far between. Always, he dreamed of his mother's house, his little hamlet on the outskirts of Saigon by the river, and, of course, his sweetheart, who had long ago married and was already a mother of three. In dreams, in reveries, Quang stepped off his ship with gifts in hand and shouted out to all the people he knew and loved, but in reality, the gifts, bought and wrapped, stayed locked in his cabinet, and, since there was no real peace, he never returned.

One day on a beach in Reunion, a lush green island with waterfalls and gentle luring waves, though he was already late and should have been heading back to his ship, Quang kept on walking. Far down the beach, Quang saw a little makeshift restaurant with coconut trees and thatched roof and, though he really should have been getting back, he headed for it. A dark-skinned, elegant-looking mademoiselle greeted him with a bright smile and gave him the menu. Conch and fish, he had plenty, but as Quang scanned the menu with the boredom of someone who had eaten too many exotic meals, he saw at the bottom of the page a word that caused him to sit up and stare: "Fo."

Remember, you have to learn to be patient. It takes cooking all night for a broth to be ready in the morning. Skim the surface for scum that boiled to the top, make sure the broth is perfectly clear, yet its taste should linger.

Dawn in her memories: she stretches like a kitten on her bed next to the large French window on the second floor. It looks out to other balconies, eight houses in all that share a leafy and mildewed courtyard. She hears the solemn sounds of Buddhist chanting from Old Lady

Muoi who lives across the way. In her memories, the wind is always cool and supple, and her curtains would sway just so, and the smell of sandalwood incense, fragrant and holy, along with her mother's complex aromatic broth from the restaurant downstairs, would fill her nostrils.

On the balcony to the right, Toan, a boy her age, is already up, diligently practicing his martial arts. She can hear the dull, thudding sounds that the impact his feet and fists make against the sandbag that hangs from the eave of his roof. If she peeks, she can see the beads of sweat on his bare shoulders, his stomach rippling with abdominal muscles in the early light. Sometimes their eyes meet for half a second, and it would be enough for the boy to be completely disarmed. He would turn as red as a firecracker, and the sandbag would suffer more assaults than usual, and she would hide behind the curtain, her hand on her mouth to stifle a giggle.

Other times, Nga remembers this: wild parrots squabbling over the ripened fruits on the single mangosteen tree in the middle of the courtyard, and Mai, the servant next door, singing a song from her favorite *Cải Lương* opera while doing the laundry, her voice sad and mournful; the heat rising.

Downstairs, in the restaurant kitchen, her mother, who had risen hours before dawn, is already preparing the day's fare with the help of her two servants. Soon, the noise of the wooden chairs being dragged on the tile floor, of chatting customers, of motorcycle mufflers, of children on their way to school, will rule the world. But not now. Not yet. Now, there is only a stillness in the salty dawn.

Nga will always associate this moment with home, a sweetness in the world so rare that it can now only be had in the recalling. She can feel it with more clarity because of her unfulfilled longings, and the years. Her mother humming softly, ladles against the pots and pans, and the steady chopping sound of the cleaver on the worn wooden block, Old Lady Muoi's pious chanting, Toan's sandbag being pummeled, his roan back, and Mai's lovely and sad voice . . .

All this—her unhurried lullaby, what insulates and owns her still, even now, from an unfathomable distance.

The bowl comes to you hot, extremely. That's how the aroma reaches the diner. Imagine dropping freshly cut onions into a bowl of cold soup—you will smell nothing, a waste of all the effort.

A hot August day in San Jose at the turn of the millennium, Kevin Pham, a boyish twenty-four-year-old electrical and computer engineer working for Hewlett Packard, entered "pho soup" in his favorite search engine. The number of hits that came back was staggering: 2,883. Kevin wasn't sure exactly why he entered "pho." He could easily have entered "manga" or "kung fu movies" or a dozen other things that always lurked at the edge of his pop culture-flooded mind. But it was near lunchtime, and as he later wrote to Bernard, his wealthy ex-dorm-mate from UC Berkeley now living in Brussels, "I suppose I was both hungry and missing my mom's cooking." It was a fateful choice. For then, almost as a joke, he began a website called phowhomthebelltolls, a popular site that rated various pho restaurants in California and had an average of 55,000 daily hits. Five bowls for the best. Two for mediocre ones, and bad ones, really bad ones, got a pair of broken chopsticks.

A few months after he built his site, Bernard sent him a cryptic email:

"Dearest K.,

If you want to eat the best pho in Europe, come to Belgium. Your homeland's exquisite broth travels—to mine. Stay with me as long as you'd like, and we can make many an excursion. Besides, I promised you 'moules et frites.' Just tell me when, and I'll send tix.

Tu me manques,

Bernard"

So Kevin came to Belgium on a culinary quest—and found himself driving up a country road one sunny afternoon with an enigmatic but beaming Bernard, who intermittently stole glimpses at his profile as they drove, their black Porsche zooming down country lanes stirring up afternoon dust.

Soon they came to a small forest, then an impressive medieval castle that loomed over the hedges. "Are you sure, Bernard?" Kevin said. "It's private property."

"Just relax and enjoy the ride, would you, babe," Bernard said. "I have a surprise for you."

At the moat, standing on the drawbridge, Kevin stopped. And sniffed. It was unmistakable. There it was, that complex aroma wafting in the air—cinnamon and cloves and ginger and fish sauce and star anise and beef broth. Someone was making pho.

Bernard steered him down a dark staircase toward an enormous kitchen, the kind that could cater to 300 people, or a hunting party of yore. In the middle of it stood an elegant Asian woman in her mid-thirties, two little mixed-race children, a boy of four and a girl of seven, playing on a slide next to her. At the far corner, a blond maid was skimming the soup. The Asian woman greeted Bernard with kisses, and then she turned warmly and addressed Kevin in Vietnamese. "Here you are. I've been waiting for a long time. I thought you both got lost in the woods." Then she kissed him on both cheeks. "Bernard spoke so often about you that I started to miss you too."

The shank and oxtail bone, pick them carefully. Make sure there's plenty of marrow inside the shanks and, as for the oxtail, don't buy those that are too large, or they can't fit in the bowl for a side dish and can often overwhelm the diner. Red pepper, finely diced, in a small dish.

In Ubud, Bali, Vietnamese pho had taken on a delicate taste. Served with fresh snow peas and a wedge of lime and no other garnish to speak of, except a sprig of amazingly spicy basil, it's a delight to the visitor, especially when the waitress blesses the soup with a white orchid to enhance the spirit of the broth.

In Buenos Aires, an Argentine, who had been to Vietnam years ago as a doctor and knew the recipe, nursed her ailing husband who suffered from multiple sclerosis back to health solely on pho broth. She told the *Buenos Aires Herald* that it was a miracle cure, "but you have to cook it with absolute devotion and love and say your prayers repeatedly as the broth simmers."

In Nagarkot, Nepal, high above the clouds, an Indian hotel owner, whose grandfather used to live in Saigon working as a tailor, is known to serve pho to celebrate Vishnu every month. Though, as in India, beef is not available in Nepal and oxen meat is used as a substitute; it doesn't detract from the taste. "The meat is only a little bit more chewy, but just as good," he claims. "Plus, up here, with such clear air and strong wind, everyone, the tourists, the people in town, everyone knows when my wife and I are making pho. Even the bloody yetis."

The lime, especially, you will pick with care, the thin-skinned ones tend to be full of juice, but they rot easily. Yet nothing's more irritating than squeezing a dried-up, thick-skinned lime over a bowl of pho. Whereas a juicy, fragrant piece of lime in its prime is heaven.

The Vietnamese woman living in a Belgian castle was now a baroness, so Kevin learned. Once a high school teacher, she fled after the war ended. With a few gold taels in her pocket, she said goodbye to her mother and father and younger brother and made her way to Vung Tau, where she bought a seat on a crowded boat. In the dark of night, they set sail. A week or so later, they ran out of food and water. A few vessels passed them by, none stopped. Some people died. Though she didn't believe in God or Buddha, the high school teacher prayed and prayed. Then a miracle: a Belgian merchant vessel took pity on their ragged SOS flag and picked them up. The high school teacher was brought back to Belgium where, owning nothing, she resorted to living in the basement of a church.

She was poor, she was wretched, an exile, but she was finally free. And she was not unhappy. She did menial labor and helped clean houses and gathered wheat crops to get by. But life is strange when you cast yourself away from what you know, and who could guess what fortune would befall you from unexpected sources, especially when you are free and open to the world?

Nearby, there lived a baron, a devout Catholic and a bachelor in his mid-fifties. He had wanted to be a priest, but because he was the last of his line, his family insisted he remain a layman. Still, he stayed pious and a bachelor. One day, while the baron was praying, kneeling at the front pew and staring up at the Madonna and child, the high school teacher emerged from the stairwell of the church and, well, the sunlight streaming through the stained-glass window must have made her glow with a certain aura. And the baron lowered his gaze and followed her down the aisle and out of the stale church. They married. Now the mother of two children of noble blood, she would sometimes catch glimpses of herself as she glided past the gilded mirrors along the old castle's corridors and shudder, wondering, who is that? Is that me? Other times, when entertaining European royalty, she felt as if she was on a movie set and kept waiting for the director to yell: "Cut!"

When her maid brought out the steaming bowl of pho, and as Kevin's face expressed awe and amusement, she said, "Eat, eat," and continued to tell more of her fairy-tale adventures. Wise now to love's variations and strange destinations and its endless hunger, the baroness was not unaware that another romance was about to unfold under her table: while Kevin ate, Bernard's hand was inching across that short yet impossible distance toward his ex-roommate's thigh.

As in all kinds of serious cooking, making pho depends on intuition, feeling, and taste. The garnish must have it all to wake up taste buds: fresh basil and bean sprouts and three kinds of chili, and wedges of lime and coriander leaves. When ready to serve, bring the bowls out steaming with aroma. Watch the faces of the diners: their eyes squint with anticipation, lips curve into smiles. Their delight; your reward.

On the wall of his office overlooking the Notre Dame Cathedral in the first district, Saigon, Toan keeps a framed article he found in a fashion magazine a few years back. Among the carved jade and gold plaques that he collected over the years, it stands alone, a treasure.

The article has a catchy riddle for a headline: "Where's the Most Remote Restaurant in the World?" But it is not the answer that thrills him. No, it's the photo of a Vietnamese woman who stares past the camera lens with dreamy eyes—the face of his true love.

Once upon a time, she lived next door to him. He could clearly see her bedroom from his balcony each morning when the curtain was pulled back, or when the wind lifted it for a second or two so as to reveal his love reading or combing her hair. Toan had recovered from the devastation of war, its horrid aftermath, had rebuilt his life after coming back from the New Economic Zone, had married, found success, but he had never recovered from a broken heart. What, after all, are ideological struggles compared to love? Perhaps it is fitting that she should come back smiling to him from a black-and-white photograph, after all the years.

But where was this restaurant? In a scientists' colony at the edge of Antarctica. The article told him that Nga had married, that her husband was a famous scientist, and that among glaciers and tundras and chatty penguins, she grew bored. While her husband studied magnetic fields, to amuse herself, Nga made pho. But it had gotten so good—everyone could smell it in the colony, how could they not?— Nga ended up selling the soup as a way to buy ingredients from South America and to make more pho—not to make a profit, mind you, only to keep everyone around her warm and happy against the bitter cold.

Sometimes, in a whimsical mood, Toan looks at the photo and imagines himself flying over a sea of ice to see her. Just thinking about it causes his heart to palpitate.

What would he say to her? Everything. A million things. Like how he ran out after her that day the communist tanks rolled into the city, but he was too late: her ship had already sailed and the world as he knew it shattered. How he would have hopped on the next ship to go after her if it hadn't been for his family, his younger, helpless siblings. How he'd never had the chance to tell her how much he'd loved her.

How he'd carved her initials and his on the mangosteen tree after she was gone and punched it so hard that his blood stained them forever, and that those initials remained, if faded and stretched, as the tree trunk widened. And how, despite everything, despite the changes and the years, his love for her hasn't changed.

Nga, the soup restaurant on Pasteur Street closed after your mother retired and went back to her province. A family moved in from Hanoi where you used to live and after *perestroika*, after the Cold War ended, they turned it into video parlor and it is full of kids playing those noisy electronic games. And now, last time I drove by, it's also a cyber-cafe full of smelly foreign backpackers.

The neighborhood has changed so much that you wouldn't recognize it if you returned. I don't recognize it myself, and I live here in Saigon. But you'll never come back, I know you. Only a handful ever return to where they used to live, and then only to look and cry a little at how the old place has fallen apart or changed, and then, again, they take leave.

Nga, remember those mornings when the borders were still real and even talking across the clotheslines or the courtyard was as treacherous as crossing the ocean? Yet how I long for that world! How I long for the smallness of things. Everyone knew each other then, and leaving was only for the few, not the many.

Everything has changed, Nga. Everything turned upside down. I changed. Oh, how I've changed. I'm a father of three, a vice president of an insurance company, the first in the country. Imagine that! I insure people against tragedy, in a country built on it.

But some things never change. I think of you. I think of you all the time. I imagine you among the howling winds. What I would give to see your face again. See how you try to guess who I could possibly be, a familiar-looking stranger standing there in front of you at the far end of the world.

But if you don't remember, if you can't recall, then I will tell you. I will remind you where we used to live, the old neighborhood, the mildewed courtyard with the mangosteen tree, and the wild parrots that fought for every fruit. Maybe you would remember. Maybe you would offer me a steaming bowl of pho while it is snowing outside. And I would be ravenous. I would eat like a mad man starving for decades, and you, you with your eyes always dreaming of some faraway place, would look on with amusement and approval.

Oh Nga, it will be the sweetest bowl of pho soup I'll ever taste.

Bleak Houses

Something about the house high up on the hills, among well-manicured lawns and stately homes, that fills an entering guest with a sense of unease, something akin to melancholy. The owner had entered first without turning on the lights, and then hurried to finish up his chores, leaving the reluctant guest to stand alone at the landing, one strewn with galoshes, tennis and dress shoes, wondering if he should come in any further.

It was still bright out, but he had a hard time adjusting to being inside and thought about turning on the lights. He stood there, hesitant, when the wife appeared and greeted him. She was just as how he remembered her, despite the years: someone who makes an effort to be jovial. She hadn't aged much. But she was not smiling, seemingly distracted by the little Maltese that followed her and wouldn't quit barking. Now it pawed excitedly at his knees, trying to get petted. "Milou," she said. "Come here."

"How have you been?" she asked. A quick first glance and a struggled smile.

"Not bad," he said. He gave her a quick, one arm hug so as not to crush the little dog. "And you?"

"Good. Good. Be a minute." She hurried down the hallway with the dog now in her arms, licking furtively at her chin. "Make yourself at home," she said and was gone.

They were to drive south together, to another house up on another hill in another upscale neighborhood. A mini reunion of sorts, after almost two decades. Except on rare occasions, when they met up and said nothing much to each other but watched a few baseball games together, the husband and the guest had mostly been out of touch.

It was his first visit to the house in any case, and not by choice. He was to be picked up by the couple at the agreed upon time. But he got to the train station early. So he took an extra-strength Tylenol, then texted his former best friend to say he was willing to wait for a bit at a nearby bar.

But the friend texted back almost immediately and insisted on picking him up. Then he showed up at the station in a pair of shorts and a T-shirt. "Sorry, bud, we're running late," was what the guest was told on the way back to the house. "It's a dinky little place in a glitzy neighborhood," the husband added. But upon seeing it, the guest realized that this was insincere. True, the house did not stand out in the tony neighborhood, but it was well-kept, its lawn trimmed, the windows sparkling. The furniture was fashionable, with a dark granite coffee table, and on the walls, antique woodblock prints—Vietnamese dancers and clowns and children in various poses—framed in black wood followed one another down the hall in an orderly pattern. He recognized the art as from Hanoi, his mother's hometown.

While the couple prepared themselves, he took to wandering. He made himself familiar with the house. After all, he got permission from the wife herself.

Built on the side of a ravine, the house had three tiers. Two flights of stairs down to the patios below from the upper deck. At the very bottom, in the back, was a workout space, in semi open-air. There were weights, a pull-up bar, jumpropes. It explained his friend's youthful physique, middle-aged with graying hair, yet lithe, a slim waist and muscular chest and arms.

He started to go down when he felt pawing at the back of his legs. Milou had escaped and found him again.

"At least you're really happy to see me, aren't you?" He leaned down to pet the dog. "Too bad there isn't any adventure for you."

They descended together to the second patio. And there, in silence, he leaned against the wooden rail and watched Berkeley, its campus, the bulk of his youth, bathe in the golden light of late afternoon. It's an extraordinary feat that his friend now lives above it, and if he stood at a certain spot, he could see a partial view of the Golden Gate Bridge, and beyond it, the ocean.

They had been best friends since high school, and then in college they became lovers. The two continued to have girlfriends, but whenever they could, they got together. It was a secret. It was unspoken. A time of AIDS and uncertainty. And when they graduated, his friend moved to the East Coast, and soon thereafter got married. Both were refugee boys from Vietnam, both from the same neighborhood in Saigon. Both loved French comic books, *Tintin* especially, and *Asterix et Obelix*, and had gone to the same country club after school—and still, even now, they sometimes texted each other in French.

After the breakup, for a period of a good decade, he thought his wounds would never heal. He'd had many relationships since then. Having hurt others, especially those who fell in love with him just as deeply as he once did, and by recognizing his inability to reciprocate on the level that they needed, he learned, slowly, to let go and to forgive. It was good, besides, to be friends with all the exes.

The friendship was only recently renewed, and much through the effort of the former best friend, who wanted to make amends. But they had decided not to visit the old battlefield after their reunion. "Let bygones be bygones," his friend said. "*C'est compris,*" he replied. "*Je m'occupe de mes oignons, et toi les tiens.*"

And they laughed. And that was that.

But now, the couple had finished dressing. The husband called out to him. So he carried the dog back up.

"There you are," said the husband. "I thought you got lost."

"Indeed, what a big house," he managed, "and a lovely view too. Congrats."

But before departure, their son must be greeted.

"Of course. By all means. Let's meet your precocious child." After hearing so much about him, he was curious.

Downstairs they went, but this time from the inside. Following the couple, he sniffed perfume and cologne in the dark as he descended. The air felt congested. The guest felt as if his asthma was coming back. He checked himself: no wheezing, no tightness of breath. He almost laughed out loud: the tightness in his chest was due to his holding his own breath. So he breathed in deeply. Breathed out deeply. His lungs were clear.

Finally, at the end of the hallway, in what he figured was a study, sat a young teenager facing a computer screen with his back to the adults, his headphones blocking him from hearing his parents. A swordsman was busy fighting monsters.

A black-and-white ceramic mask hung on the wall above the computer. He recognized it. It was his gift to his friend when they were sophomores in college. He'd bought it on the fly while on a family trip to New Orleans. A half-black and half-white ceramic mask with no facial expression, it had stared back at him when he first saw it on Decatur Street. He couldn't resist. He knew then to whom it belonged. He spent the bulk of his savings for the trip, nearly $100. It surprised him that it had survived the years.

"Ken!" the father called out. "Ken!"

By the third try, the boy removed his headphones and slowly swung around in his chair as if the air was made of water. On screen, the swordsman stood ready beside a destroyed house, katana raised high in the air. Handsome. But not as handsome as his father used to be at that age, at least not in the way the guest had remembered it.

He had dreaded this moment: the running into an old lover's family, the quiet confrontation, the subtext. And he half expected this moment as something out of an old fantasy—that the son would resemble the father so much that he would feel a pang of longing, of loss, but it turned out not to be the case. What he felt was something else: that he was intruding, that there was something about the family dynamic that he didn't understand, and he'd made a mistake by agreeing, at his friend's coaxing, to attend this reunion at which everyone was expecting him but in which he hadn't invested much. And it ended up with him entering a foreign domicile that left him feeling ill-prepared.

It was now hard to say, facing an old lover's child who he studied with mild interest, how he felt, everything about the past seemed so distant and opaque, yet ever-present. For years, he held a gaze toward it that was both nostalgic yet bordering on the mythic—*were they ever that vulnerable, that passionate, that young?*—but trying to see the past now was like trying to see the bottom of a lake in turbulent waters.

The introduction was brief. The boy smiled, listened politely as his parents bragged about the guest's accomplishments—a journalist, an author, world traveler—as if here was a living example of what the boy, too, could be in adulthood, if he so wished.

The boy nodded. "My dad talked a lot about you," he offered shyly, studying the guest's face.

"Oh? I blame it all on the lunacy of youth."

The boy laughed. The wife scowled. The friend shook his head and said nothing, though he too tried not to laugh.

And then just like that, the adults retreated to the living room upstairs where the couple promptly excused themselves once more. They had forgotten to select a bottle, and now they needed to find one from their collection that would be appropriate for the occasion. The guest had brought his, which was left in the car; a rare burgundy with an earthy aroma and faint floral smells of roses, violet, and raw, freshly-picked cherries.

On the living room couch, waiting yet again. He felt restless. The guest sat looking out to the hills near sunset. Shadows began to shift, a dance on the walls. He listened to his own breath, felt his heartbeat. Far off, and muffled, he heard the couple's voices ebbing and rising.

An argument? Then, again, silence.

The sun, all but gone now, still somehow reached the house through the distant ridges from across the bay, illuminating the room. Nothing seemed solid in the gloaming. He closed his eyes again. Memories jumbled, jostled, and danced—his childhood in the old country, his many lovers, his mother holding him as a child, the sounds of bombs, rain, heavy rain on tin roofs, like horses galloping, then memories of tenderness with the man who was now in the other room but at an impossible distance, lost and yet relived countless times.

Like images from a magic lantern, one by one, they turned into shadows, into shades, and that old impulse rose up and gripped him once more: to fly somewhere, to go to another country, to a foreign place, experience something new, be lost in another's flesh, even if knowing that to run away from the past is no way to escape it.

When he opened his eyes again, darkness had taken over much of the house. In the dying light, something flickered through, and he saw a lingering shadow out of the corner of his eyes. When he focused on it, it began to take shape. A young woman. She stood by the sliding door to the patio, slender and delicate. She was looking out to the bay. She seemed to be waiting.

Then, just like that, the gossamer apparition merged back into darkness.

He blinked. His hand instinctively reached up to touch his left shoulder. It was where his best friend had bitten him the last time they made love many years ago, which left a little scar, though it had long ago faded. "Remember me," the lover had then whispered, and they both wept. Or was he the only one who wept?

He wasn't scared. He'd never seen a ghost before and wasn't quite sure whether what he just saw wasn't something he himself projected. What surprised him most, however, was that he was neither shocked nor frightened. No, it was the way his fingers lingered and rubbed over where the scar used to be, as if feeling the pain anew, its enduring power.

"Hey, bud, we're ready. Got the vino. Let's go."

The wife offered him the front seat.

The guest quickly turned it down.

No, please, I am bad at navigation. He knows what a terrible driver I am.

The wife stayed mostly silent as they drove, easy jazz on the radio. He and her husband chatted. Mostly of their college friends, those who prospered, those who did not, the divorces, the adultery, whose kids got into Ivy League schools, and those who had died so tragically young; one by drowning while swimming, what a shock!

They went further back. The two reminisced about their childhood in the old country during the war, the gated community they grew up in; they marveled over how they were but a few blocks from each other, knew people in common, yet hadn't known each other. And yet, ended up in the same high school in the new country, then the same university.

"By the way, can you believe my next-door neighbor back in Saigon found me?" the husband said. "I was what, like nine, when I left? She was eight. We were best friends, and we used to play in the alley in the back. Turns out after we fled, she snuck into the house and saved some of the photos we left behind, just before the commies took over and gave it away. She said she wept for days afterward."

He'd just got an email out of the blue, the husband said. He was animate. Somehow—so many years had passed!—she found his contacts through a mutual friend, and in her email, he saw images of himself as a young and happy boy. He saw images of the *Cercle Sportif* where he used to swim and play tennis. He saw the old Saigon, and it all brought back sweet memories. "She basically said I needed to go meet her in Phoenix. It's where she'd resettled. That is, if I wanted the photos back. Maybe I'll go. Maybe I won't. I want those pictures back though. But it's emotional blackmail."

"Yeah, it is," the wife agreed. "Flying that far for old photographs. She should just mail them."

The husband laughed. Then he said at length, "I was her only friend, you know. She wept for days after finding out that my family and I left."

Heck, we were evacuated. We didn't have time to pack, let alone say goodbye. Sorry, no can do."

"Well, you can do so now," the guest said quietly. "Or try."

Then he added, as a joke. "But I just now realized that you broke hearts even *before* you made it to the good old US of A."

The wife suddenly laughed. Yet it sounded more like a cough. The husband glanced quickly at her. Then he checked his friend's face in the rearview mirror. But the guest looked out the window, pretending to be fascinated with the rolling hills.

An awkward silence ensued, and the husband fidgeted with the volume, letting jazz smooth over it.

He will entertain. He will enter another grand home on another plush hill and compliment the hosts on their good taste and fortunes. He will make them laugh. He will love their expensive wines, will listen attentively to stories of how well their children have fared in school, or how well they played the piano and violin, will amuse his old classmates and their spouses with stories of his own adventures, which he'd told and retold at various gatherings. He will make that little speech about the past and the present, a pithy lesson of making the best out of sadness, the variation of which he gave a couple times at college commencements. They will laugh and murmur their admiration for his bohemian lifestyle, his articulation, shaking their heads thinking how extraordinary that the once-shy boy transformed into an intrepid world traveler, a reporter at that, just like his childhood hero, Tintin.

The Burgundy Magnum in his lap felt heavy, but he kept cradling it, his knuckles intermittently turning white as they drove amicably into the night.

To Keep from Drowning

"Quit it!" Rose said in that plaintive voice of hers, nasal and whiny, when harassed by Ben, the middle boy. "Quit! Or I'll kick your ass. I swear."

"You? You and what army?" Ben said and continued to pat her head and mess with her hair. Then he yelped. Their mother, trailing behind, had caught up and jabbed him hard on the arm with her thumb. Even with his parka, it still hurt. "What the fuck, Ma!"

"Good," their mother said breathlessly. "I do again."

He jumped out of the way as their mother reached out theatrically with clawed fingers, and the girl laughed. "Yes! Ma, you do again. Give Ben exactly what he needs. Fucker!"

Nhung, their mother, glared at her for swearing as the boy took off down the trail to find Lou, their eldest brother. All about them were trees and shrubs and the sounds of waves crashing against shore while seagulls circled above, calling out to one another.

Nhung hugged herself. It was a warm day, but she was cold. She struggled just to walk on her purple ballroom dance shoes, her ankles swollen. "Ohm mani, mani, mani, pedi, pedi, ohm," she hummed. That was her favorite phrase, which sounded like her morning Buddhist mantra before the family altar that housed the two Buddhas and images of her dead mother above their fridge. Both a joke and a prayer. How many hands and feet had she scrubbed, washed, massaged, and how many nails painted, this last decade? She couldn't possibly know. Thousands, surely. So much so that when she dreamed, she dreamed of hands and nails and feet, and rarely of faces. Hands and feet, feet and hands, what a life!

Despite the fresh air, the girl felt queasy. She took out a brush from her purse and struggled against the wind to comb her long, flowing hair. The bus ride had been too long, and she felt nauseous throughout; the way that damn driver stepped on the brakes, it was as if he hated his passengers. It didn't help that the ripe odor of a homeless man mumbling to himself a few seats down made her want to hurl. Ben hid his face in his jacket's collar and sporadically made clownish faces at her, but she'd half hoped he and Lou would go and chase that bum off the bus.

It was midmorning when they started out, walking some distance from their rundown apartment complex on 12th Street in Oakland. They took BART to downtown San Fran, a familiar enough trek, but this time, they didn't go to gawk at the high-end stores around Union Square or shop at Dress For Less and Ross south of Market Street. Instead, they boarded the 38 Geary heading west and got off on 47th Ave, thinking that it was the end of the line since the driver stopped and went out to smoke and everyone else got off. Not quite yet the ocean, but since they didn't know their way, Lou said, "this way," and veered the family north in the park.

The boys walked with a kind of swagger typical of kids of their neighborhood, making themselves much bigger than they actually were, taking up extra space, as if walking on unsteady ground. Tall for Vietnamese, they made themselves bulkier by wearing down jackets even when it was hot, hands in pockets, elbows and shoulders jutted out. Mother and daughter followed slowly behind.

Lou carried most of the heavy stuff in his oversized backpack—the soft drinks and tea thermos, a Tupperware of fried rice, dishes and chopsticks and spoons. Ben carried offerings in his: paper money and paper gold ingots for the dead, incense, a couple mangoes and pomelos. She, the youngest, had a camera dangling from her neck, what her father left behind, and carried the lightest load: a basket of daffodils and roses.

She, the youngest, who was very good with directions, was otherwise distracted. She was too busy checking her phone every other minute.

Aaron, call me, please!

• • • •

The outing was rare. Their father drove them to Tilden Park eight years ago for a picnic, but that was before things fell apart. It had been for her mother's birthday. She remembered her mother blushing when he, in a rare moment of affection, kissed her on the cheek.

Yet, in the middle of the week, here they were trekking toward the sea. For a picnic.

They walked for nearly twenty minutes but the ocean, though it sounded near, was nowhere in sight. Lou's windy path took them through a dark grove of cypress, and then they found themselves on the edge of a golf course. Sporadically, the faint sounds of sea lions barking reached them. Then their path trailed back toward the city, which caused Lou to curse.

Ever since their father went to jail, Lou pretended to know everything. But Rose knew better.

She saw how he struggled with his college homework.

"Rose, stay with Ma," he ordered when she started sauntering down the trail.

"Why don't you?" she sassed.

"You want to get beat?" He raised his fist.

"Lou, you hit," their mother said, "I kill you."

Lou softened up: "I'm gonna look for the right trail. Stay with Ma."

But he didn't come back. And now Ben was gone, too, looking for a path to the sea. Left behind, mother and daughter walked slowly, a basket of wilting flowers between them.

Rose hated her mother's pace. Walking with her was like sinking into the earth. Though she did not resist, she became nervous when her mother grabbed her arm and held on. The touch was rare. The arm-holding freaked her out a little. They were walking slightly upslope and on uneven ground, and her mother's breathing was ragged.

"Damn, Ma? Your asthma again?"

"Yeah, okay," Nhung said and stopped walking. "Rest five minute."

"Let's sit over there on that bench," Rose suggested. "And let me carry that old lady purse."

"No, I carry," the mother said and shifted her shoulder away, as if afraid of being robbed. But her grip on her daughter's arm tightened. Rose grimaced. Stubborn woman. Her grip hurt, the nails digging in. She would feel bad if she left, though she really wanted to join her brothers. No doubt Ben was smoking a reefer right now, out of their mother's sight, and wolf-whistling any cute chicks on the trail.

She checked her phone.

Aaron, call me, text me, please!

• • • •

"Size matters." Lou, who had friends in the gang and a black belt in karate, taught his siblings how to fight. "You look bigger than you are, you get into fewer fights," he declared.

"And when you don't have no choice?" Ben asked.

"Go up fearless. Be a warrior, till the end."

Lou had stolen a couple cars and shoplifted. He often carried a Glock. He smoked weed since he was eleven. Though he didn't exactly join, he flirted with the neighborhood gang. He had the OJC tat on his left bicep and had spent a short time in the county jail. His mother had threatened to kill herself if he'd ever get locked up again after she bailed him out, and that very same night, had half-heartedly cut her wrist to prove it. It was theatrical, but it did the trick. Lou wept. He used salt and lemon, and after many tries, managed to rub some of the tat out.

He taught them how to play poker with real money and not show emotions with their faces, their eyes. He also taught them how to fight, leaving them black-and-blue in the aftermath and cursing at his back. Their mother, working ten-hour days at Danang Nail, was rarely around to scold or beat him with her bamboo feather duster like she used to when their father was still around.

"Stare at your opponents. Don't show fear in your eyes."

• • • •

"You think you so pretty, Asian bitch?" Rashanne Halls in seventh grade had once asked. "Thanks for noticing," Rose replied, "jealous much?" Which led to a hair-pulling fight and some punches thrown. But that girl's rhetorical question echoed. She checked herself in the mirror the next day, trying to figure out how to use her hair to cover her black eye; that bootsy girl packed a stinger. She did stare at Rashanne unflinching. Still, her answer to the mirror was hell to the yes!

"Rose, call me Rose," she told her friends in eighth grade, the name derived from her Vietnamese name, Hồng.

She told Aaron the same. She was in love. She was slender and had just turned fifteen and was a beauty, her curves forming. Rose checked her phone every few minutes as they walked, which annoyed her mother. But she couldn't help it. Aaron hadn't texted for over a week, nor called despite her messages. The only time they talked was when she called Whole Foods and he practically hung up on her. "I'm working, Rose. Don't call this number. You want me to lose my job? Talk to you later."

What went wrong? It drove her crazy!

• • • •

On the bench, Nhung's phone started to ring, its dial tone set to "La Vie En Rose." She opened her purse, searched for it, and after some fumbling, found it. Three messages from Danang Nail! They must be wondering. Somehow she'd forgotten to call and let them know that morning. But at this point? Fuck 'em. Let it ring. Already gave them her lungs, what else do they want? Kidneys? Liver? Left arm?

She studied her daughter, who paced back and forth on the trail in front of her, staring intermittently at her cell phone. The girl wore tight jeans and a short T-shirt that showed her navel. Her dark hair shone bright in the sun.

Nhung wanted to cry. What would Rose do without her mother? She wanted to hold her daughter so badly. But as usual, she resisted. To show that much love is the same as hurting the person you love when you are gone. She knew this painfully so: nightly, praying to the altar, how she missed her own mother, who died too soon.

"Ma, you need to re-dye your hair," Rose said as she looked at her mother through the camera. "The gray roots showing." Clicked.

"Ohm mani, mani, mani, pedi, pedi, ohm," Nhung mumbled. "Please protect my children."

• • • •

Only Lou remembered the boat ride that ended with their grandmother and uncle dead. He remembered being pushed and pulled to shore. He was only four. And Ben was one. Rose hadn't yet been born. Hell, he didn't even remember the refugee camp much, just dreamlike images of flapping tents in the wind. How it all went down was never clear to her, the story fragmented in her mind. She never asked, only eavesdropped.

Seems there were some Thai pirates, and it was their mother's older brother—Cau Hai—who jumped in to protect Ma and Aunt Mai from being raped. He was chopped down by a pirate with a machete. But Ma and Aunt Mai were saved when Grandma, on her knees, begged and begged.

And Ba? Ben asked.

Ba didn't do shit, that's how he survived, Lou said. Maybe that's why he's such a loser now. Ma said he was near unconscious because of thirst, but whatever, man.

And Grandma, how'd she die?

Grandma? She was OG. She died saving your skinny ass when that boat capsized near shore. Hauled our asses then lifted you out of the water. Then boom, heart attack, falls backward, then she was gone.

What the fuck, Ben said. Grandma did that? She's badass, gangster as fuck.

Lou slapped Ben on the head. Hard. Don't you ever say that word when you mention Grandma, you dumb fuck!

What! But you . . . then Ben knew better and shut his mouth. He saw it in his head, not in actual memory but imagination—being lifted out of the water and into his mother's arms. He rubbed his head and laughed. It's all good, he said.

Rose didn't ask any questions. A loser! Was he? Secretly, she was glad he didn't do shit. Would have been chopped down with machetes if he did; she would never have known him. Going to sleep each night, she still hugged the stuffed monkey that he gave her for her eighth birthday. He worked for a time as a broiler at Sushi Heaven. He brought home delicious stuff when he was still working. Too bad he got into debt at Oaks Card Club and got beat up by collectors and had to borrow money on top of taking all the family's savings, including Ma's jade earrings and necklace, and selling the Toyota Corolla to pay it all back, or else they'd break his skinny neck. Then, when the guy at work asked for his money back, it led to a fight and a stabbing, and he was sent to jail. Nine years for assault with a deadly weapon!

They moved to the one bedroom after that. Mother and daughter shared the one bedroom, and the brothers shared the living room, bunkbed style, and it was bus to school and shopping malls, bus or BART to work. To see Ba, you needed BART and two buses, all in all, six or seven hours roundtrip. After a while, the trekking to see him proved too difficult to sustain.

A loser. Maybe. But still.

• • • •

Lou hated the secrecy. All the years in Danang Nail on MLK, sucking in chemicals. Who else but he to take her to hospital? But when the results came, "No, Lou, don't tell!"

"What?"

"Give them peace, okay?" Nhung kept saying this as she cried in his arms. They were outside of the hospital waiting for a bus. "Nói tụi nó má bị xuyễn!"—Tell them, it's just asthma.

"Fuck! Not okay! Ma, this is not good!" Lou said, but he kept his mouth shut, hid the X-ray and CT-scan and the doctor's somber prognosis after the biopsy. It was stupid. How she gonna lie when chemo treatments started, all the hair falling? Wear a wig?

All he could see were the kids weeping. Her coworkers cried at Danang Nail Salon. They even collected money for copayments and such. Aunt Man, her sister, who lived in Denver and sent their mother money from time to time, wept upon the news. She promised to take in the youngest, meaning Rose, worst comes to worst.

His grades weren't good. In fact, he might have to repeat two courses, which really meant he needed to forget about the whole college thing. But even to drive for UPS, it helps to have an AA. He didn't think he could last. Last week, he felt like kicking Adam Johnson's ass when the guy "accidentally" bumped him with his backpack, picking a fight. Get a grip, dweeb: you're not in high school anymore, bad blood or not. No one cared if Lou was a tough guy who was stabbed twice and survived, nor did it matter that Johnson survived a drive-by. Besides, it would be his second fight in a year, and though he ain't afraid of nobody, he's got to focus on graduating. Or get a full-time job soon. Washing dishes part time ain't gonna cut it. Fuck! Fuck! Fuck!

Lou found the sea. He stood near the edge of the rocky bluff overlooking the ocean, panting. He had been walking fast. Now he had to get the rest of his family to follow. But first, he picked up a rock at his feet and threw it as far as he could toward the waves.

He was very young, but he remembered. His uncle tried to protect Ma and Aunt Mai and was chopped in the neck, the blood spurting. He could still hear grandma's scream, which shattered his insides. How his grandmother managed to get on her knees begging, begging, begging until the pirates turned away toward some other girl. He remembered the muffled cries that girl made as she was being raped— high-pitched and weepy.

Lou resisted the impulse to take out his gun and shoot at the ocean, at the invisible pirates. Lan, that was her name, which meant orchid. She survived, even though she went insane in the camp afterward, mumbling to herself, and the kids called her "Lan Khùng"—Crazy Orchid. How often did he fantasize of killing those Thai pirates, shooting them in the groin, the neck, between the eyes?

• • • •

Rose studied her mother. Something's up. This trip to the sea was something else. The flowers alone cost $17. The nail business hadn't been good.

Whenever they had "giỗ"—death anniversary—for Uncle Hai and Grandma, it was a quiet thing. Just a few incense sticks and a couple of mangoes for the altar with Ma weeping and mumbling her Buddhist prayers to the dead and all the Buddhas.

"Old ladies so cheap only want just pedi, no mani, no spa, no feet massage," her mother complained. "They so fat they no reach. They do their nails but no can do toes. Thanks to gods, or I'm out of job."

So why spend so much? Ma's been sick too. Coughing every night even with herbal remedies and inhalers.

She stared at her cell again, hoping that sheer willpower alone would cause a text to appear.

Or did their mother know? That Ben, he always knew everything. Did they know that she was dating? Was this one of those situations where she was going to be lectured and yelled at?

God, she loved Aaron so much. The way he kissed every part of her; she'd die if they broke up.

The way he cooed Seal's "Kiss from a Rose" drove her insane. It's an old song, he told her, but he memorized it just for her. Those tattooed arms and that delicious smile, the butterfly kisses. Her body heated just from recalling. Aaron wanted to "take her to town," to which she joked, "Boyfriend, I already live in The Town." And they both laughed, both Oaklanders, born and raised. It was thrilling, this secret: with an older man, their first date—her birthday—was going to the zoo, then eating at Oliveto's.

Her grades were good, so what's the big deal? She was getting straight A's, including geography and history and precalculus. She'll be taking two AP courses in junior year. Not dumb like the boys. She's attending Charter High, after all.

Okay, they did have unprotected sex a couple times, even though she didn't want to. But she'd put a stop to that. She's not stupid. Now they're careful. Her period hadn't come though. It's freaking her out a little bit. She will have to find out. Marilyn Loveless, her best friend, will help her get the necessary pill. Shit, Lou will kill Aaron if he finds out. Ben might be even worse, that snake in the grass, always smiling.

She rubbed her flat stomach. Aaron! Call me!

A tall teenager gave her a smile as he approached. Tourist from Europe, maybe, the lankiness, the elegant haircut, the expensive watch and white tennis shoes, that light blue sweater draped over his shoulders, its sleeves tied like a scarf. She pretended not to notice, but her body tingled. He was stripping her with his eyes. Her lips curved into a half smile. She tossed her hair as if to air it out after a hot shower.

He slowed down as he neared, smiling.

"G'day!" he said.

"Hey there!" she said. An Aussie.

She was going to say more but knew better; she felt her mother's eyes on her, narrowing. He walked past, still smiling. She didn't need to turn around to know that dude was checking out her ass.

It made her think again of Aaron, his kisses. They'd only been together for a little more than three months, but she knew: she was in love. For the last week, though, no texts, no phone calls. She'd shown up twice at Whole Foods, but he wasn't there.

They had to hide their love affair. After all, she'd just turned fifteen, and he twenty-two.

Plus, her mother had said so many times, "No boys. You want boys, go live on street."

Still, she knew: she wasn't done with school. And her mother would beat her with that damn bamboo stick.

"Aaron I miss you. Pls txt r call." As she texted this, her mother suddenly sat up from the bench and said something in Vietnamese. *"Hổng mày có bạn trai, tao từ mày! Mày mà để con sớm đời mày khổ'!"*

It took her a second or two to translate. "Rose, I'll disown you if you have a boyfriend. If you have a child early, you'll suffer."

"Ma!" It was as if her mother read everything in her mind. She walked a few paces further away. She pretended to take a photo of her mother with her father's camera. Nhung immediately posed and held up the basket of flowers which were wilting away next to her on the bench. Her smile was wide and fixed. But after the shots, her smile disappeared.

"Rose, I want you no dating," she said again, this time in English, a stern voice. "Too young. You study. You don't be like me, stupid, no-good husband, poor, poor, poor. All day, mani pedi, pedi mani . . . ohm!"

"Haha. No, Ma, I'll be a dentist," Rose said. Her mother had looked frail in the camera despite the smile. When she clicked, she saw something ominous.

"No mani, pedi, pedi, mani, om, for me, Ma, swear ta god."

"Good," Nhung said. "I so happy if you a dentist. You can fix my teeth and Ben too. Rose, give Lou extra novocaine. He need it so bad. Haha."

• • • •

Ben knew. The X-ray and CT scans. The biopsy. Saw them. A thief in the night, Ben was just seven when he took money from Ba's wallet and gave it to Ma when the old man was a drunken slob. He siphoned off from Lou's Bo-Bo stash without Lou knowing it. He knew where things were hidden. He knew when Rose lost her cherry. He could see it on her face. He memorized everyone's PIN by spying on them. He'd read her texts. Girl was in heat. From the corner of his eyes, he studied his sister, who was too busy looking at her phone, waiting for it to buzz. He almost laughed. He'd made sure that it wouldn't. Not from her Romeo anyway.

It had been two weeks in the making, their excursion. Ben said: "Ma, it ain't like we are going to some picnic, right? We're just going to burn some sticks for bà ngoại and cậu hai, and then we jam, right?"

"No jam, no peanut butter," the mother had said between coughs. "*Cúng rồi ăn,*" which roughly translated to, "Do offerings, then eat."

"No peanut butter!" Ben giggled. "Ma, that's rich!"

"No one rich. And how many time you see ocean over here?" their mother said, annoyed. Half of the time, she didn't understand what Ben was saying. After laughing so hard, Ben was on the sofa having hiccups. "Peanut butter," he kept repeating.

• • • •

Rose thought about her mother's question. The answer? All the time. But also, never. The bay? All the time from The Town. Always there, but the ocean? Never. Too damn far away.

Or rather, only once. She'd seen it on that field trip when they crossed the Golden Gate to Napa, a rarity for her junior high. Mrs. Thompson, the principal, even said it: "We're blessed this year with this grant for inner city youth," and Rashanne responded, "Yadada, yadadamean," which made everyone laugh and Rashanne got kicked out of the auditorium and banned from the trip. Phew! That was why it was such a fun trip.

But when she got home, Lou asked, "How was Napa?" and she said, "Stupid and lame. Like who cares about Jack and cheddar making, or how pinot grapes are picked? Give me Welsh and Spam anytime, okay, bitch!"

And he laughed. "That's hella funny, Rose."

She didn't tell him about the ocean, which gleamed under the sunlight. She didn't say anything to anyone about that moment when they crossed the Golden Gate Bridge and she, sitting by the window on the left side and thanks to the tall bus, saw a view that quickened her heart. Sailboats fluttered over a sparkling sea that stretched toward the horizon. The sun's reflection on the surface of the water at one moment lit up the roof of the bus, and she yelped and closed her eyes. The sea seemed to be made up of a trillion stars, even with her eyes closed. Everywhere in her mind, water shimmered.

Her friend Marilyn Loveless, who was listening to music in her earphones, woke from her trance, asked: "What, girl?"

"Nothing," Rose said. "I forgot to bring my damn money is all," which was a lie. Her mother had given her $10, even though the lunch was included on the field trip, which was why she ended up using it for a new pair of shades when the bus made a quick stop for gas and restroom breaks. How could she tell Marilyn Loveless that the light on the sea made her breathless?

So beautiful it freaked her out. This'd be her secret among secrets: how much she liked the taste of cheddar on a piece of crunchy baguette when they were allowed to taste it at a factory in Sonoma. And hell yes, she wanted to someday try, too, that pinot noir.

• • • •

"I work, work, work," Nhung said through a sigh as they trekked. "Never see ocean."

The sound of the sea was louder, and familiar. She tried not to cry. It brought it all back: the fishing village, the stilted house by the mouth of the river leading to the ocean, the songs she used to sing with her mother. Her long hair. Rain like horses galloping on their tin roof. Laughter with all her friends and neighbors. All of them, now long gone. Relocated, arrested, or drowned.

But the sea, so close, was calling to her now.

How did they end up so far away, with children not knowing a thing about the old life? The one not so complicated and drugged up and full of anger and all the crazy drive-by shooting? Fish and rice and going to temple and praying and getting married and having children and worshipping your ancestors. But of that life, across the waters and long ago, not even one photograph survived.

Nhung, which meant velvet, a luxurious name for someone who never got a proper education past sixth grade. Never got to take more than two ESL classes that first year. Then, after Rose was born, all work. Did she even tell her children the name of her village? She couldn't remember. Do they even know her father's name, a dignified man who did nothing wrong except that, being the village chief, he worked with the previous government and was taken away by the Communists after the war to the reeducation camp. He never came back. She wanted to tell them all about that past, but they never asked, and most of the time, she didn't want to relive her own losses. She regretted it now.

"You've seen enough for a lifetime, Ma."

"No, I want you to see too."

• • • •

Her brothers were nowhere to be seen. What's this trip about, anyway? Some kind of intervention? Did Ma know about Aaron? "Taking a day off from school and work for Land's freaking End?"

But her mother's coughing fit interrupted her. She felt stupid as she watched, the woman's face an expression of pain. Her mother had been coughing for a while now. Sharing the same room, waking up night after night to the coughing, Rose felt it was worse than asthma. But her mother assured her that was what the doctor diagnosed.

Maybe it's something else? She reached out and tried to break that invisible wall between them, to massage her mother's back, but couldn't. Something, an unknown force, kept her hand from touching her mother. Instead, she reached into her own purse and looked for cough drops. The inhaler wasn't working. "Ma, do you want a Menthol? I brought some with me."

She wished she could tell her about Aaron, who would have gotten along with her the way he did with all those older ladies, which was to say, much better than she did. He was polite. Aaron knew all about herbal remedies, working at Whole Foods and wanting to be, what was it? "A homeopathic doctor." He knew exactly how to make you laugh. She'd ventured in for the first time looking for a treatment for asthma with money Ben gave her. That was where they met, in fact, in the middle of the herbal aisle of that fancy store. And he sneaked out a bottle of elderberry the next time they met—my gift to Mama.

She kept thinking of Aaron holding her last week when they went to the park. She felt so at home for the first time, safe, in his arms, the warmth of his skin. When she cried and talked of her parents, he wiped her tears. But now she couldn't see his face. All she saw was her mother's, and it was grimacing.

• • • •

"Land End. What this?" Nhung stared intensely at the wooden sign. She had recovered from her coughing fit and was sucking on the menthol.

"Land's End?" Rose said. They finally got a text from Ben to tell them to take the trail to the left.

"It's just the name of this trail, Ma." But her mother seemed perplexed. Rose tried again: "Okay, let's see, um, *hết đất rồi*—like, no more land, the end of land." Her Vietnamese was rusty at best.

"This is where America ends and the Pacific Ocean begins. The transcontinental railroad ended in Oakland. A hundred years ago, you'd have to take the steamboat from where we live to San Fran, probably takes all day. The Chinese got chased out after they finished the rail. Maybe all the way back to China." She'd done her homework. It was her best effort, she thought. "Not easy to get to California back then until the railroad connected the continent. Before that, some people had to eat other people when they all got snowed in up near Tahoe."

That was her best report freshman year, the story of the railroad and Chinese coming to America, earning her an A+.

But her mother was visibly shaken by the explanation. Nhung's eyes searched westward beyond the hedges for something. *"Hết đất rồi!"* She repeated the phrase to herself. Then she added: *"Mất nước luôn!"* — no more water as well! And with that she started to cry.

"Ma, what's wrong?" But Nhung just kept shaking her head and wiping away tears with the palm of her hand. Rose opened her mouth to say something else, then stopped. She just realized what her mother was saying. It had nothing to do with railroads or Chinese. Or California for that matter. When you add *đất* to *nước*—land to water, in Vietnamese—it means mud, it means rice paddies, ultimately, it means country.

• • • •

Ben lit a reefer and leaned against a eucalyptus tree. The wind in his hair. Good shit. But where the fuck was that Lou? He could see the ocean from where he stood.

It was windy, hard to light up. Took him four tries, with his parka over his head like a tent, for the fire to catch. "Fuck, what kinda weird picnic is this?" he mumbled and took a drag when a hand reached out from behind and took the smoke from his lips.

"Fucker, who told you to do this here?" Lou said.

Ben didn't say a word as he studied his brother taking a drag before snubbing the fat reefer out against the tree trunk and putting the rest in his pocket. Someday he'd like to kick Lou's ass. Or stab him in the eye. Or pistol whip his head. Dude's an idiot, taking the wrong trail without consulting the map.

But without Ma, Lou'll be guardian. So, note to self: can't kick your legal guardian's ass until you're eighteen or until Ba is released early for good behavior. Maybe pick a girl by then—Lucy or Caroline—get hitched, a real job. He knows he's smart, just can't prove it in school. He'll figure something out. Maybe move to Denver, to be close to Rose and their aunt.

"You better stop selling too," Lou said. "Word's getting around. Anything happens to Ma or Rose, I swear . . ." He looked toward the ocean. "And if you get addicted, well, they'd better shoot your skinny ass before I do."

Ben didn't say anything. He was making good money. He's been selling more than weed. Special K, vitamin E, some vikos. He won't touch the hard stuff. No crank. No go-go juice. No horse. Mostly party, hug drugs. And he's been careful. Only in school and among friends. The welfare ain't doing it. He was buying food for the family, for himself. The way he ate? His mother would have to work three jobs. Plus, he's been giving spending money to Rose. Told Ma he's got a job working for a small construction company after school. She was the only one who believed his boldface lie, or at least she never questioned it.

So what the fuck? Lou's jealous, that's what it was.

Lou seemed to be in some place. Ben studied his brother, whose eyes were all sadness. Lou was trying to hold it together. "Anyway, go back and lead them here. I found the trail—it's just seven minutes that way to the beach. I'll put out the spread."

Ben didn't say shit about the scans. He put extra money in Ma's Danish Delights cookies where she hid some of her tips from Danang Nail. She kept that tin under her bed, as if that was a good hiding place. He knew too: Rose will fall apart. He gave her $40 to go buy asthma remedies, knowing full well it wasn't going to do much good.

A mistake: he knew about Grocery Boy. He followed them a few times. He even sold some candies to the dude a couple times at a party. Things didn't look good. GB was not who he pretended to be. Too hot, too bothered, too fast. He let it go on too long.

Ben took some photos of them kissing. GB lives with his mother. Ben not only got GB's number, but GB's mother's too. He even took pics of texts between him and Rose on her cell without her knowing. Her passcode: GB's birthday, which was available on Facebook. He got it on the first try. So he put an end to it last week: just a quiet holla, rattling the name of the manager of Whole Foods and mouthing "statutory rape" and "jailbait" and presto! GB's skedaddled. All done. GB promised: he'll never call or connect with Rose again.

Anyway, there's the nuclear option: tell Lou. But that would mean Lou'll get in trouble, too, knowing unrestrained Lou.

He knew mean-ass pimps. He knew girls sold, beaten. Belinda, for instance—in school one day, gone the next. Only to end up working for that mean SOB Richard on San Pablo and 61st, all beaten some morning, staggering in the fog, like a shadow of a ghost, cold on high heels and in her miniskirt, sometimes high on crack. He gave her a burger a couple times. Told her she could escape but no, she was too addicted, too afraid.

Ben wouldn't tell Ma about Grocery Boy though, nah, she didn't need no extra stress. And Rose'll recover soon enough, a little heartbreak'll do her good, especially when she moves to Denver and gets her head on straight. Aunt Mai will take Rose in. With two daughters of her own, Aunt Mai can't take all three but definitely can take one, and Rose's her favorite. She got along with the little cousins, who adored her. No worries there, he's got Rose covered.

He got Ma a jade bracelet, too—not the one Ba bought for her in America but then pawned off; that one's long gone—but one better, after selling his third batch of candies. It'll be his gift for Ma's birthday next month. She'll be buried with it.

He'd saved up over 6g so far. His thinking: Rose'll need some money when Mamma's gone and she's shipped to Denver. And Lou will need money for a funeral.

At least he won't be a foster, 'cause Lou is eighteen now. That fly-ass car will have to wait. "Rose, take Ma and go down the trail on your left. 10 min walk till it splits in 2," he texted his sister. "I'll wait there 2 take u 2 da promiz land. Lol."

He stepped behind a tree and took a leak then, with time on his hands, took out his special plastic container, hidden in the lining of his parka. He picked an E and popped it in his mouth.

He put on his earphones . . .

Yeah. If the picnic's gonna be dull, this candy and Eminem'll make it slapping.

. . . .

Never much of a walker, and now with her ailing lungs, Nhung bent down, out of breath, palms on knees, panting. She watched her swollen ankles and chafed toes, and the purple color shoes, sinking into the soft earth, and wanted to laugh. What the hell was she thinking?

She cursed herself. Stupid, not much of a think-ahead gal, which was why she was where she was. Didn't know it was going to be uneven ground? Ignored the pain in her lungs and the coughing until blood came out? Why did she allow that good-for-nothing husband to sell her car and now she and her children suffer? If she were alive, her mother would beat her on the head for being so stupid.

"Om mani pedi om," she whispered under her breath. "Please save me, Quan Yin, Buddha, and Mr. God. Please, protect my kids!"

"Ma, you ok?"

"Yeah, yeah, Ma okay," she answered without looking at Rose. After the breather, they resumed walking again, she now leaning on her daughter's shoulder. She tried to show composure as she slouched toward the direction of the sea, her lungs burning. It felt like she was drowning on dry land.

"Where the fuck is he?" Rose said—they were at the point where the path split into two. "Ma, he was supposed to wait right here."

There was a path to the left that would probably lead to the beach. Ahead of them was a rocky bluff and some large shrubs, and of course, the sea. "Where!" she texted Ben. "Ma's sick! Can't drag this 2 long."

"Down here!" he texted back. "Go off path, get on rocks, look down & u c."

"Ben's below," Rose said to her mother.

"Oh, good," Nhung wheezed and gestured her daughter forward. "Go check."

Rose felt her mother's hand on her hair, her neck, gently pushing her. She put down her flower basket and took a few steps, tentative at first, then stepped off the trail and onto rocky ground, going past the shrubs toward the bluff. The land rose slightly closer to the edge, the rubble crunching under her feet. She walked a few more steps, and the sea came into view.

"Ohm mani pedi pedi mani pedi pedi ohm," Rose said. The moment seemed to call for it.

The wind buzzed in her ears, her hair flew.

"Om mani pedi mani pedi ohm," she said it again. The water sparkled, its surface dancing. Below, near where waves lapped against shore, Lou, kneeling on a blanket, was putting mangoes on a plate. At that angle, he looked so much like their father that her heart skipped a beat.

"Rose!" She turned toward Ben's voice. Lower right. He was standing with arms akimbo on a large rock, looking up. He was grinning. He still had his earphones on. He was rocking. Even from this distance, she could tell: dude was lit.

But her gaze turned back to the sea, the air smelled of dead fish, kelp, and salt. She squinted, and it stretched so far that it blurred where it became sky. She raised her camera. She studied the sea through its lens. Focused. Clicked. Refocus. Clicked.

Behind her, Nhung closed her eyes. It was all she could do to stay standing, her body shivering, her throat and lungs burning. The purse strap pulled her shoulder down. *"Phù hộ, phù hộ, ông bà ơi, Phật bà Quan Âm ơi, làm ơn, ông bà ơi, con cháu!"* she whispered—protect, ancestors, protect, please, merciful lady Quang Yin, please protect the descendants.

Her mother's face that last moment came back as if carried by the waves. Nhung managed to stand on the sand then, and with one hand still gripping Lou's, she reached back to grab for her second child from her mother. When she looked up, her mother was grimacing. They had stared at each other while Ben wept hysterically in her arms, seawater burning his eyes, his nose. Then Nhung watched as her mother clutched at her own chest and fell backward into the water.

"*Ma'oi*," Nhung whispered. She felt dizzy. Jumbled images filled her head. In one, her mother stood against the waves and guided the entire family to shore. In another, her mother dissolved into foam. The sea roared in her ears. "Ohm mani pedi . . ." she managed.

Lou meticulously arranged the mangoes on a plate and took out sandwiches and the tea thermos. He tried to ignore the sounds of the waves crashing against the shore. "Grandma, please help me graduate," he mumbled. He had never prayed to his grandmother before. Or rather, he couldn't remember the last time he prayed. "Please," he said, staring at the plate of mangoes. "Please, keep us all safe. Keep us safe." He felt stupid saying it. Then he mumbled, "Take me if anyone."

Rose shivered. Cold wind. Land does end here, and abruptly. Crops of rocks jutted out toward water, and the constant roar of waves and wind numbed her mind. Her hair billowing. All she saw before her was an unspeakable vastness.

She took a photo of Ben dancing on the rocks. Lou on his knees, spreading out the offerings. She took one of the sea.

Then she paused. Ma crossed this freaking thing with Ba and Grandma and Ben and Lou, and Aunt Mai? And this . . . this vastness swallowed Grandma and Uncle Hai? Ma so boss. Was Ben heavy? And how did a starving, thirsting woman carry two children to shore, and manage to lift them above them waves? She wanted to turn around to look at her mother to confirm.

But she didn't turn. She felt she had to look straight ahead. The sea hypnotized. Looking at it was like staring at a distant future.

"Stare and don't show fear," Lou had said. But when she stared at him at home, she had to look away. It wasn't that she was afraid of showing her fear, more like a fear of betraying what she saw: behind his show of fearlessness was sadness and anger. But she was staring now. She stared so hard her eyes watered and then something flashed in her head. A big house on a hill. Her brothers, older, with their wives, their kids running around in the big garden. She saw herself older, too, sophisticated, her hair tied up in a neat, polished bun. She saw in a large kitchen, a turkey roasting, pinot noir poured into long stemmed glasses. She saw herself humming some sweet lullaby.

Lou finished with the setting out of the offerings. He looked up to see his sister standing against the wind. He wanted to yell at her, damn girl so careless, standing so close to the edge, but something about her posture shut him up.

Nhung had been staring at her daughter's back. She was beyond exhausted and shivering in the wind. The air felt thick. Her lungs on fire. She opened her mouth, trying to say "I love you," but the words lodged in her throat, burned like coals and came out as faint hisses.

But her daughter's laughter jostled her out of herself. A clear, joyful sound. It came to her then. It surprised Nhung that it took her all this time to accept it. Her mother wasn't grimacing before dying. No, it was, upon seeing the rest to shore, a victorious smile.

It's her house, Rose decided. She saw it so clearly that even the ocean before her faded. Her life, the future. She'll make it real. She almost reached out to touch that vision of herself when she heard Ben from below.

"Come down, little girl," Ben yelled. "You won't fall. We'll catch. Ha ha."

He had taken his headphones off. Everything about him was so lit up he could barely focus. The grass, the rocks, the bushes, the clouds— all shimmered, glistened, and shone. The wind and waves roared in his ears. He was watching his sister intently. The way he felt right now, he could bend the winds.

Then Ben, the maniac, spat that familial phrase like a love song.

Ohm mani mani pedi Jump Jump baby . . . Jump, Jump . . . Ohm, Ohm . . . Ohm baby.

Behind Rose, Nhung crumbled to the ground.

Rose raised her arms dramatically toward the sky, as if gathering strength.

Ben, still buzzed, saw many arms, all with well-manicured hands, forming an iridescent arc about his sister.

"As if," she yelled down to him. "Ain't gonna fall, dude. Gonna fly."

The Shard, The Tissue, An Affair

Not that the glass shard had any business with the sole of his foot; nevertheless, it made itself familiar. And it was an unending story of how he teased and squeezed and how it refuted his negotiations. But finally, the shard—so small, smaller than the tiniest teardrop—was retrieved, and he, pained still, examined it for a brief moment against the halogen lamp before flicking it to hurl like a comet out my window.

On my bed he sat, a teary-eyed Shiva, his wounded foot raised in the air, kicking, kicking.

I should have swept carefully. This was no way to welcome a poet. I should have mopped, waxed. Something. Now, I watched as he wiped the wound with a tissue paper and felt awkward, like a caught voyeur. But then he looked up and smiled. Come here, he said.

We had seduced each other over the phone and via emails a year before we actually met. An essay of mine had found its way to his part of the world, and he took the initiative of sending me an email full of compliments. I replied, thanking him for his kind words, and discreetly enclosed my number.

He called.

We talked.

Mostly of home, of our tropical Vietnamese childhood. He named for me seasons half-forgotten, our childhood fruits, fruits eaten in stealth and ecstasy. Remember the green mango? Sweet and sour and crunchy, eaten with salt and red chili pepper or even fish sauce, hidden under the student desks while an old geezer of a teacher droned on. And the durian, loafs of yellow brain eaten with glee by the entire family after dinner, fingers digging through a split thorny shell the size of a skull, family brain surgery, that's what it was, a ceremony of shared flesh. And what a smell! Rotten flesh fragrance, its pungent aroma remaining for days in your hair, your nostrils, your breath. And the milk apple, green and purple outside, milky white inside, to be eaten after siesta, its cool and smooth texture sliding against your throat like sweet ice. Afterward, washing the milky sap off your lips, scrubbing real hard, and seeing how raw they looked in the mirror, as if from too much kissing.

I, in turn, recounted for him the flame trees that blossomed in the courtyard of my elementary school, red and green, glowing to the point of blindness under an unforgiving sun, its black fruits, hard shells that fit perfectly in a child's palm, turned into swords for the boys to duel with. I recalled a summer villa veiled in a cloud of red bougainvillea by the ocean in Nha-Trang. The way I slept in the afternoon on the second floor, soundly, insulated in my parents' rhapsodic laughter, which echoed like shattered crystals from room to room (and how I loved the roaring sound of waves out the tall French windows that made me dream of tigers). My favorite childhood smells: the sea, of course, with faint suggestions of kelp and dead fish, ripened rice fields at dusk, my grandmother's eucalyptus ointment to ward against evil winds, the sweetness of sandalwood incense burnt by my pious mother nightly.

On the phone late one autumn evening, I whispered, Read me a poem. Out on the bay, the foghorn wailed mournfully. A poem, please.

I don't know, said he. You were supposed to send a photo, remember?
I'm sorry. I'll send one tomorrow. I swear. Poem, please.
Hmm . . .
Read, please.
Leaving

Mother burns pages of albums
wedding day, first child, father's
funeral, Tet
quick, she says, hurry, pack,

prepare
we'll sail away
down river
to sea . . .
Saigon in April
A season of smoke

His poetry went on to speak of a perilous journey, one full of wonders and griefs.

So I took my chance: will you come for a visit?

To your city? he asked.

Of course, I said. By the sea. You can see sailboats every morning out my window. Hear the cable cars go rumbling-clanging by. Feel the sea breeze on your skin, taste its salt . . .

To fall in love is to have one's sense of geography grafted onto another's, no matter how tenuous, so as to form a new country. I saw Houston in my mind, a city of strip malls, grand old homes and gleaming glass-and-steel skyscrapers that coexist cheek by jowl. He, in turn, imagined San Francisco with its Transamerica Pyramid poking the blue sky, windblown hills the color of ember at twilight, sailboats gliding on the bay like playful white butterflies; he imagined—and I could tell this from his voice—that there was freedom somewhere in the next valley.

Alright, he said, I'll come. In December, at the beginning of winter.

Then he stepped on the shard. And had trouble walking the next day, his new boots, bought a week before, unyielding, his dye-stained socks kept sliding downward inside. He walked the city, my city, with the slightest hint of a limp.

We were otherwise chirpy as songbirds that first day. At lunch, we held hands under the table at Cafe Claude while I introduced him to friends, and afterward walking home, we broke into an old folk song about rice harvesting, a song learned so long ago and so meaningless now that neither one of us knows its lyrics entirely.

Day two: to Carmel. I drive, my hand resting sporadically in his, Cesária Évora cooing nostalgic ballads of love. Last night, under a flapping red awning of a stucco apartment building somewhere on Russian Hill, we kissed and I, impulsively, beckoned him to move in with me. He stared out to the dark water and contemplated the offer. Then, before I could speak, he kissed me again and shut me up.

He contemplated the sea, a glittering sheet of silver lamé that stretches back to the past. It must be strange for him to see the Pacific once more, so long hidden from him in Texas, the ocean a reminder of that terrible flight on that crowded boat full of refugees from Saigon. He relives it all once again. He sees the small of his mother's back as he huddles her children in the corner of a dark and crowded and stinking hull. He wanted to take her place so that she could rise to the upper deck and smell the fresh air, even if only just once. But she never did. That journey, she kept her lioness vigilance over a sickly brood. It was him who begged for water, who gathered bad news. It was him who told them how blue the sky, how vast the sea.

His siblings are grown now, his mother well past middle age and half crazed, and she, like a benevolent spirit, still needs to watch over him, over them, lest he would somehow lose all purpose and meaning, though how he yearns for freedom, god only knows, a nightly defeat.

He turns to me then, the wind in his hair, the sea a blur in the corner of his eye: I want to. I really do.

Day three: Something has changed. A shadow has flown across my window, a movement in the stars. The initial delight of recognition shifts to the fact of too many details; we fall into routine. He sleeps on my favorite side of the bed, my left shoulder hurts from the weight of his handsome head. The way he throws the scarf over his shoulder vaguely bothers me, and I can't say why. Sometimes he has this sad look, a poet's melancholy, I suppose, and is unreachable. He wears it too often, like a geisha his powder. I look at him now insulated in sadness and wonder how his books could possibly fit in my apartment when my shelves have no more space for V.S. Naipaul's collected works?

Day four: He discovers an unfinished poem on my desk, an ode to his beauty. He says nothing, but I can tell he doesn't really like it. It's not jealousy, it's the fact that I have moved into his "territory," even if to woo him. Something in his sigh I recognize too well: it's claustrophobia.

Day five: Or rather night. Rain. A chorus of remembrances. Fifteen years and he is tonight as he was then, a moist-eyed boy standing in the refugee camp watching his mother hugging his sickly brother, her youngest pup dying of pneumonia before her eyes. He is drunk, not from the alcohol, but from trusting, and grief. He stares out the window and speaks of leaving, of wanting to leave, leaving his mother, which is impossible, leaving his siblings, who have already left him, leaving Texas which he didn't care for, leaving everything, his memory, his sadness, what owns him.

We buried Little Binh in Guam. Around the grave we stood and sang his favorite song then left his plastic dog on the mound until the rain washed it away. My sister went back to look for the grave last year, but she couldn't find it. Some mornings, my mother stares out the window and cries as if it had just happened last night.

Listening to him, I suddenly am also overwhelmed by a particular memory. It was in summer of 1973, a year after the ARVN and Americans recaptured the city of Quang-Tri near the DMZ. I had visited it with my father via helicopter, a rather strange excursion. The city was destroyed in the recapturing, reduced to piles of rubble by B-52 bombs that left deep holes that, after the monsoon, turned into swimming pools for the children who survived. I walked about. Behind a broken window of a house sat an old woman. She sat as she must always have, with the ease of years, but she stared out to nothing now, the old neighborhood gone, and the wall that held her window was the only thing left standing of the old house. I remember waving to her. She did not wave back.

Day six: I want to tell him, the angel sleeping on my shoulder, that it's strange how love between two exiles can be thwarted by the hunger of memories, that Vietnam remains, in many ways, an unfinished country between us—even now, body to body, lips to lips.

Day seven: She needs me, he says. You're lucky. You're free.
   And therefore, I thought, utterly alone.

On the way back from the airport, it suddenly occurs to me how the tiny shard came to be there on my floor. A thin crystal vase that held a dozen white tulips toppled over one windy evening last spring. I remember holding the flowers upside down, drunk and out of breath, a lake of sharp crystals lapsing at my feet, water dripping from the grieving bulbs like melted snow.
   A month, and still no news. His phone is disconnected. This morning, I found the wrinkled tissue dotted with dry blood under my bed, my own shroud of Turin. He is so far away now, hidden across time zones, cocooned in requiems; I walk barefoot in my apartment, hoping another shard would pierce me too. But I'm not made for such a thing, alas, and must resort to keeping under my cool blue satin pillow the blood-stained tissue, remnant of an uneasy dream of communion whose yearning is long.

Love in the Time of the Beer Bug

Good Afternoon Folks, have I got a doozie for you.

It's Rrrrrrumbling in the Bronx, part deux.

It's Tango with them Bojangles . . . redux.

Or . . . maybe, just maybe, given our terroir, Regrrrets in the Sunset? I'll let you decide. But for sure this is it. With little tremors up and down the coast for years, the Big One is finally here.

And just like Elvis, we're all shook up.

Also, as preview, you can hear crying and shouting, albeit muffled, for the last few weeks through the walls. I caught some on Voice Record, and you can listen here at this link below . . . beerbugneedshug.com.

I also have with me Grandma T, who is slouching slowly toward Bethlehemzheimer's, who sits worshipping her *opium du jour*, better known as Korean Soap Oppa-Oppera—and, well, folks, she's rooting for her champ, distractedly, of course.

Mind you, she can still spit verse like the best of them.

"Hey Grandma T, what do you think of D-Day? Who's gonna win? Does it matter?"

"Who's Klingon? I am Leon."

"Okay!"

"Small-town marriage leads to baby carriages, baby."

"Nice. Grandma. Who's gonna let you listen to the best beat when I'm gone?"

So folks, how do I know for sure it's D-Day today? I eavesdropped on Grandma T here and Janice. Since there's nothing else to do while SIPPING. And until Goddess Vaccina comes down from the heavens with her flaming needle to pierce the beer bug like a rabid dog, I will continue to spy on everyone for lack of better things to do.

Folks, you can thank me later.

Yesterday afternoon out in the garden, under the honeysuckles, Janice dropped the bomb on Grandma T. As if asking for blessings and permission, and thinking they were alone, she said rather loudly— "*Không chịu đựng được nữa, má à. Con như một người lạ với Stan á. Con biến mất từ từ trong mắt của ảnh.*"

Google-edited translation: "Can't take it anymore, mom. I'm like a stranger to Stan. I'm disappearing slowly in Stan's eyes." (Yeah, Jan, tell that to someone with AS and AD and whose fabulous mind is literally disappearing into dementia. Jan is many sensible, splendid things, but folks, sensitive is not one of them.)

"*Ráng đi con,*" Grandma T said. Google Translate: "Endure my daughter."

Then, just like that, broke into one of her Eilish-ish moments: When you sleep, I do not know where you go.

"Oh, Ma," Janice said. "Oh no. I don't like that."

Round 1

With no further ado, in the corner by the stainless steel sink, I give you the lithe 5'3", 122 pounds, forty-three-years-old but still in her prime, Janice da Menace Nguyen, who is also known as Lioness Who Devours Her Young Especially if You Sass, though before she was Janice, her Vietnamese name was actually Hiền, which means gentle, so go figure. You just don't mess with Janice though. You just don't. I mean, good God, folks, go gently into that good night, or watch out, Janice will be your worst nightmare. If she had to tuck you in and you didn't want to go to sleep, and you wanted, say, your standard Disney fairy tales, she would tell you in Vietnamese, something close to "The princess died. The end. The Prince never came back. He's an ass, that's how charming he really is. So sleep now or I'll cut you, you little shit."

Okay, I jest. But folks, that's how it felt for a child of five staring at his future of at least three failing marriages by middle age with a sizable beer belly and barely enough of a budget for much-needed therapy and, not to mention his overdue hair graft installment, going by the look of Stan.

Speaking of whom—in the opposite corner, drinking his third stale cup of Java at the breakfast table in his bluish-gray Tartan boxers and classic wifebeater, folks, I give you the Slouching, the Grouching, Stan Wisniewski. Stan was the Man, but at fifty-one, 6'2", and 227 pounds, which is not healthy, but hey, what do you expect from someone whose best buds are Budweiser and Pringles? Stan lost his mojo from too many cocoas, and long before the beer bug blows-blows.

He's mostly off-grid these days, folks. But if you must, you can usually find him in his man cave most evenings doing his thing, which is basically watching ESPN or lesbian porn and jacking off. But lately he's on his laptop trying to either get unemployment or PPP loans. Considered self-employed with some 1099s from last year after he got bought out from the car dealership on the cheap by his partner, he's supposed to qualify. But the freaking EDD website isn't working for people like him. He's frustrated. He's cursing. He qualifies for some EIDL grant, but he's not at all sure if he should apply for unemployment, SBA's PPP loans, since what business does he have to protect now but bruised pride?

Janice is just frustrated. The way she's chopping that free range chicken to make pho for tonight, still in her yellow *Kill Bill* à la Bruce Lee tracksuit, you'd think that chicken is guilty of sedition.

But say what you will, Jan can cook. And she brings home the bacon too, which has been the bane for her opponent, who used to be the breadwinner. Now, she's wearing the proverbial pants as well as a Bluetooth earphones, so she can dictate to her assistant who is also WFH due to the beer bug.

She's making chicken stock and more important stock options. And now, I mean right this sec, after setting the chicken soup to simmer, she's roasting ginger and onion. Soon, she's kneading the dough for an apple tart, though she's long been rolling in it so to speak, and please excuse the cheap puns, it's desperate times here.

Over the years, Janice gained ground and confidence, made more dough, and then when she got her MBA, got promoted to sales exec at Salesforce, got into stock investment after night courses, and then bam, the power balance completely shifted.

But folks, with all that tailwind, it's not an absolute win for Jan. Slumping and slumbering, Stan's still got some good right hooks and crosses. Jan won't get out of this totally unscathed, and she knows it.

No doubt, he's practicing some fine lines down the cave just for this very day. And you know what they say about a cornered rat? He'll bite, if he has to, the cat.

They tried everything. Marriage counseling. Family therapy. Family Buddhist retreats (her idea). Slightly unctuous Catholic priest sermonizing (his). Yes, it was Janice who footed the bill for therapies. After about three years of on-again, off-again of the $300 plus a pop at the shrink, plus one Zen meditation retreat too many, everyone more or less agreed on the one thing: the only inner peace to be had is without the other. Which was why when the beer bug came, this household was already well-versed in social distancing.

But again, I digress. I am also distracted. 'Cause Leia just texted. She wanted help with homework. We are technically part of a study group of five, but the others are morons. And I'm the fall (for her) guy: "JJ, What do u make of LitToC, maybe the Love as illness theme?"

What Leia wants, Leia gets . . . so I'll BRB, folks.

Okay, sorry about that . . . GDB—Girl distracted boy. But yo, I'm back. :)

Folks, the fight started in the kitchen in the early afternoon. They had been sizing each other up after a silent lunch, but kept their social distance, that is, six feet apart and just slightly out of each other's swing's reach.

But now they're ready. Inside the ring, Jan jabs.

"If you can't figure it out, go ask Johnny."

Stan the Man turned Stan the Underdog mumbles something inaudible while staring at his laptop. He's pretending his best not to hear her. He's king of the slip and roll.

Sure, he used to be a looker. Sure, he still got Nana Kasia's blue eyes, but the raven black hair now is more craven pepper and salt, a retreating carpet toward the temples. Had a great smile too, if you look at the young version's photos, especially in the wedding album. But, well, search as you may folks, you would better find the spotted owl or the snow leopard than that winsome smile on Stan's face in the latter half of this decade.

Stan is one-eighth Navajo and one-eighth African American and three-quarters Polish but not at all lately polished. Heck, folks, to be honest, he's getting up there with being a candidate for being a victim of the beer bug, which freaks out Jan, who is a jogger and fitter than a twenty-two-year-old. Her regimen now is reduced mostly to the treadmill instead of her Ocean Beach regular jog for fear of crazy white Karens and Kens, and it frustrates her. She doesn't want to run into haters who blame the beer bug on people who look like her, and she hates to mace the mofos and stream the event on YouTube.

Yes, a woman warrior true and blue, she carries mace and an iPhone 11 when she's out and about. She can live stream your racist ass in the first half of a second and kick it in the second.

She's taken seven years of tae kwon do and, until lately, taught self-defense workshops at her workplace during lunch breaks.

Yeah, she even has a YouTube channel. Meet Janice.

In short: don't mess with Jan.

The beer bug got us SIP and Jan sipping martinis, and as the weeks wear on, occasionally flipping off Stan behind his back.

They've been clashing. He's been losing. But what else is there to do during these trying times but to duke it out?

"If it's beyond you, ask for help." She's jabbing again.

The dough for the tart is suffering under her iron fists as she casts slight glances at her crouching opponent.

Stan looks up, pretending to notice her for the first time: "You stay out of this. Keep drinking. You're good at it."

She ignores him. She goes to the edge of the kitchen to the living room.

"Johnny, what are you doing? Why are you wearing shades in the house?"

"Playing *Fight Night Champion.*"

"Again? Go help your dad."

"'Kay."

"No, keep playing, champ," Stan yells. "Don't need help."

"'Kay."

"Stop mumbling. And stop playing games. Don't you need to Zoom or something for class?"

"Already did."

"Leave him alone. Jesus, Jan. He's tuning us out, that's what he's doing. Can you blame him? He already got accepted to Yale, what else do you want? His grades don't count much anymore."

"Help your dad. He can't figure out how to apply for unemployment. He didn't make much, but he has some 1099 from last year, so that should help him out with the fed grants and PPP."

"Jan, don't patronize me. I'm warning you." Stan's voice is rising with each word.

Now she starts cursing using Grandma T's language. I know most of what she's saying, thanks to Grandma T's tutelage.

Folks, she's saying, more or less, "Fuck your mother. I'll let you eat shit."

A familiar expression among the traditional women of Vietnam, surely.

But no. Not at Stan. Not yet. Right now, it's directed at the bottle of fish sauce which she just took out of the cupboard and found out that it's almost empty. Pho ga will not be the same.

A run to Irving Ave is in order. She grabs her mask and the alcohol wipes pack and stuffs them in her purse, then bounces out without responding to Stan.

Folks, shit happens in many a marriage. Often, love quickly turns into things that are not love: in Jan's case, it's mostly contempt. Longing soon turns into dissing, affection wanting defection. If at the beginning of a romance, love is a series of long-winded love letters (I should know, I read a few of Jan's letters still in Stan's shoebox sent that summer when he worked in New York), then at its end, well, it's a series of abbreviations. Jan went from I miss you so much to MYO and MIA. And Stan went from I love you with all my heart to AWOL.

Truth? The party was over a while back. They get into different people. Let's just say Jan's all about "disruptive technology." And Stan is, well, he's "legacy industry." And legacy's fucked. It's slouching toward bankruptcy while the Beer Bug bites—all those trophies for selling gas-guzzling vehicles are on the mantel but for naught. EV's future is now.

And it's worse, far worse, now that we're all SIPPING.

Jan's like WFH. Stan's has that "WTF am I doing here?" look.

And I'm like SMH and praying for deliverance.

But NVM—never mind, indeed, folks, never mind. I digress. Given the circumstances, there's no better time to fight, tbh.

So . . . Round 2

She's baaack! With three bottles of fish sauce, with some ginger and fresh noodles to boot, and—not that it's exactly needed for pho, nor is the other bottle empty, exactly—a sizable bottle of Bombay gin.

Back in the hot-getting-hotter kitchen, Janice is clearly frustrated. She's fixing herself another martini. She tastes the broth after spooning in some fish sauce then sips her martini again, all the while scowling and casting sharp glances at her opponent, who hasn't moved since she left.

She can no longer wait. She dashes over to see what he's doing with his laptop.

He slams it shut.

"Back ... off ..."

In Vegas, the bets are 17:1 Jan v. Stan—and they're being generous. But it's not a sure thing for Janice. He's still got some good hooks and crosses. She won't get out of this unscathed, folks, and she knows it.

Yes, they've been clashing. Yes, he's been losing. But what more does he have to lose now? For all we know, he might be saving some ancient, secret fighting techniques and go all out. Going down but going proud, you might say.

Or, if worst comes to worst, he can always bite her ear when they clinch, and not in a good way.

Janice backs off. She mumbles something, but it is not inaudible from where I am. But here's Stan's repartee: "Well, if you showed affection, the kids might learn to love instead of fear you."

It's a straight hit. The martini swiveled but didn't spill. Underdog he may be, but Stan still knows her vulnerable parts.

Janet puts down her glass. She picks the porcelain tureen, a gift from Nana Kasia as part of a set from Neiman Marcus on their tenth wedding anniversary. But she's not scooping or skimming, or rather she's smiling her "I'm-in-control" smile, which is razor thin and barely shows any teeth.

"I feed them and pay for them to go to the best schools. Stan, I help them with their homework. If you raise them simply with mere affection and fake compliments and now with your 'hard to access' unemployment benefits, we might have to eat hugs and cereal for breakfast in some trashy trailer park."

Ouch.

"Well, don't you underestimate love and affection." He is clearly flustered.

"I wouldn't know, Stan. It's a rare commodity between us."

Then: "Oh, on that same topic, I want a divorce."

Oh shit. There. Finally. I mean, wow, she said it. I mean, she . . . fucking . . . got . . . it . . . over . . . with. The D word.

"What?" He knew it was coming. But he clearly isn't prepared for a sucker punch non-sequitur.

"Of course, you can keep your Ford Escape."

Ouch. Another right hook. Stan staggers. Which is to say, the stale coffee is gulped hurriedly to calm nerves. She knows how to hit, and hit hard.

"Jan, let's talk calmly."

"Sure. Since I bought it, I'm keeping my Tesla."

"Who wants that shitty electric car anyway?" He regains his fighting stance. "You can go kiss Elon Musk's ass if you want. But it's overhyped. That stock's way overpriced. I'm shorting it. Your followers are going to curse you for recommending a buy when it's a sell and take profits."

"Sure. Short it as much as you want, Stan, with whatever cash you have left, from your dead dealership. But I think it's best to sell the Ford stock before it goes to pennies. What is it now, $3.99 a pathetic share?"

"You know what? You're being really nasty. Fuck you!"

She turns to look at him fully. Her eyes narrow.

"Witty. Not that you're capable of getting it up, but no thanks. Which is why we need to bury this dead canary and get out of the mine. My lawyer already drew up the papers. I'll send it to yours."

He pushes himself up from the table, steadying himself to leave.

"Our tenant at the Infinity will move out after next month. Since it's furnished, please stay there until we can figure out the paperwork."

Stan stares back at her. He has the look of someone who sees the light at the end of the tunnel and realizes that, well, it's Jersey. "Jan . . . that's a big loss of income . . ."

"But an immeasurable gain to sanity . . . Surely when you make all that crazy rich money from shorting Tesla-my-ass-la, it's the least of your worries."

Okay, folks, that's a one, two, three combo.

It's like giving him the finger while rubbing salt into his wounds at the same time. This, folks, after giving him the boot. At work, she's known to be excellent at multitasking, but it's awesome to see it when she's WFH.

See Stan age. See the air go out of the Irish Zeppelin. He slumbers slowly out of the kitchen, laptop hugged against chest, and retreats back down to the man cave.

Now, Janice, alone, is crying silently into the crook of her arm.

But then Bridget, her assistant, calls. And just like that, she's back in top form, fingers pressing on her Bluetooth earphone, as if ready to beam up to some brighter future. "No, no, Bridget, Bridget, dear, listen, the logo needs to go on top of the second page as well, and the product descriptions need to include . . ."

But folks, here's the Eternal question, which burns like lighter fluid on the mind of Generation Y, a question that won't stop for any peasant or pedestrian: What? What is Stan, who is mad as hell at her, but so dependent on Jan, gonna do without her?

Well, uhm, let's get a second opinion.

Let's WhatsApp Stacy. Folks, she's been clued in, in Boston. She's online.

Me: Yo! Jan + Stan big blow out. D-Day declared.

Stace: Wow! She keeping da Tesla + house ++?

Me: U expect anything <<?

S: Poor Stan. Good tho 4 both. Like now they can have new lives, ie . . . fuck other people.

Me: That'll be good. Jan needs it. Stan might already. Not during SIP tho. Btw, he said "Fuck you" 2 Jan. Like #shocker like #wow.

S: #Wow2. That's rare. Stan's no mean drunk. Speaking of fucking, you & Leia, hello? What's up?

Me: She provoked. He's caffeine hi. She tiger-wived him in2it tho.

Her 2nd martini. Re: Leia: A FAQ but MYOB. And no, not yet. Maybe never. Lol.

S: #Tigerwived. LMAO. BTW did u tell them about Cal? Or Yale? We'll be neighbors if Yale. Decided yet?

Me: No they're SITD. Jan wants Cal for sure 2 save $$, + cuz it's EECS? Yale + Creative Writing? Not so much. But why tell her anything? With beerbug tho, maybe going nowhere.

S: Fuck - another season with Jan & Stan #shitshow? STBU. EECS is hard to get and you'll make bank after Cal. Either way do it in 3 yrs, save Jan $$. #notworthittodrag in beer bug era. How's grandma?

Me: She's like into Eilish right now: She wants to bury a friend.

S: Bitch—Stop putting your damn headphones on her nothing-(As) perger ear like when she's napping. I'm serious! She's so smart. Like part of her brain's genius level w/ music, the other part like #Arcticmelting?

Me: Right?

S: + hadn't she buried enough back in NAM, including Grandpa & Uncle B? Then raising Ma and Aunt D by herself?

Me: Right? But seriously how's Stan gonna do w/o Jan?

S: Trust me . . . I know Stan. Stronger than he acts. Stronger than u give him credit 4. Stans needs 2 explore. YOLO right? Anyway, Got2go

Me: 'K. Stay safe

S: U2 babe. TTYL. Mask on!

Round 3

Ding. Ding. Ding-A-Ling.

Like clockwork, roughly thirty minutes later, there he is, meandering up from his fortress of solitude with a new T-shirt, jeans, and what seems like a new attitude. I would call it his negotiating face.

Which is to say, he's showered and shaved, and now with a combover. "What's cooking?"

"Pho ga," she says in an even tone, the American way, without the diacritics and without looking at Stan. She's been looking at her iPad. "Every week, I make this dish, Stan."

"Oh yeah . . . hey, Janice. Listen, sorry I lost my temper before. But Jesus, I mean, what happened to us?"

OMFG. Sorry, but I have to interject here. I mean is this like for real? Ha ha, I mean who writes this fake news afternoon special? I mean, let me take this photograph of them in this light in case it is the last time that they are exact stereotypes from a straight-to-Netflix romcom. 'Cause it is just like a bad movie. It is just like a wrong song. Adele #forgiveme.

Maybe with the combover, he doesn't give a fuck that he's also a walking cliché?

Will Stan do a *Streetcar* scene in his wifebeater next? Can he shout "Beer Bug! Hey, Beer Bug!" while searching for Jan?

Will Tesla's stock go to the moon, and will Space X go IPO?

Or will Tesla go down the drain with its ridiculous P/E ratio like the bears have been saying? Jan knows it's the former. If she has to play Stella, she'll prob call it "An Electric Car, with an innovation technology that significantly alters the way that consumers, industries, or businesses operate, named Tesla, to be fully automated in two years. And please hit the like button."

"How about I move down the basement for a few months? That way we can rent out the condo and have some extra income and give each other a breather." Sly fox. He knows you can't rent condos out for a few months at the Infinity. It's a rule: half a year minimum, preferably the entire year. He also knows nobody's renting right now. They're fleeing to good-old Sacto, or Tahoe and beyond. Besides, Stan's more or less already moved down into the basement last year.

Jan's struggling for words. You can't attack someone who just apologized to you. You need to at least try to pretend to consider his offers. You also know that she's trying hard not to laugh—out loud.

There's still some affection reflecting in her gaze, folks, plus a modicum of amusement, but mostly, after the need to laugh subsides, it's clouded over by pity.

The truth? She's already made up her mind. She's got the upper hand.

"I know we got off on the wrong foot the other night. I know I can be an asshole."

"Wrong foot?" she says, sounding incredulous. She studies Stan as if he's just crawled out of his dark watery cave looking for his Precious.

"It's just . . . Stan, listen, I have nothing left to give."

"You think I had it good? When we started, who worked double shifts so you'd get that damn MBA?"

"Jesus, can we not go over this over and over again? Who's been paying for your fancy meals when you use that Visa card the last few years even as your dealership sank? Who bailed you out of debt while paying tuition for Stacy?"

They both crouch again, guards up, claws out.

Folks, they are just sparring now. After landing that major D-Day blow, Jan's sizing up her opponent. She's still looking for a vulnerable spot. But not hungry for a KO. The deed is done. Now, as long as she wins . . .

"Those were business lunches, and you know it. You know I was hoping for a restart." Say what you will, Stan's stubborn, he won't give up until the bell rings.

"Stan, we can't just go over the same things again. You gave. I gave. Now it's just me giving and you just taking . . . I mean, why does it have to be two Michelin star restaurants? Jesus, if it weren't for this virus, you'd still be going out and eating and drinking us into the poorhouse."

"Well, if you really want to know, I never really did like your Vietnamese cooking."

OMG. N to the O. No, no, no.

Mr. Referee, wherever you are, stop Stan the Grouch this instant! That was way, way below the belt! Surely, a mistake. You can't take that shit back! And frankly, folks, I'm also offended. It's like a hate crime. Worse, when he used the second person possessive to spell his own doom.

Jan stiffens up. Eyes narrow. "Well, go boil some potatoes and cabbage then, you fucking freeloader!" With one swift push, she sends the pot-o'-pho clanging to the floor, and it lands like one humpty dumpty bitch on its side, spilling its broth and parts. Stan jumps out of the way, showing some fancy footwork, finally. Still not satisfied, Jan throws the tureen in his direction and it hits the wall behind him, hard, shattering on impact.

"What the fuck, Jan!"

Even if he'd saved that insult for an emergency, the equivalent of Tyson ear-biting Holyfield, Stan must realize that space between them—now filled by a lake of delicious chicken archipelago and with the steam rising lazily from the floor toward the ceiling—had become an impossible chasm, and ain't no bridges can ever be built over it, ever again. It's the end.

Our pugilists now stare sheepishly at each other, both silent, both wary and subdued.

Grandma T turns from the Opppa-Opera. "Hey, what's for dinner?"

"A long unhappy marriage basted in its own resentment, Grandma."

"Okay! Smells very, very good!"

Round 4 . . .

There might have been a fourth round, but he doubted it, not with that mess that Jan made. In any case, he never bothered to find out. By the time he got back from his food run, it was cat-yawn quiet; his grandmother snoring on the couch; Jan and Stan having long-since retreated to their private corners, the kitchen floor sparkling, laudably clean.

Who could have thought the innocent chicken pho was going to get insulted by the husband then KO'd by the wife, not to mention the shattered porcelain tureen to forever serve as a marker of their disunion?

Another round of fighting, given Jan's coup de crass, would be overkill.

The teenager walked. And walked.

Where they lived, 35th and Rivera, was but a mile or so to the Ocean Palace. When he reached it, the sun hung low above a calm Pacific. But the OP's dimmed lanterns and the setting sun reminded him of an empty temple in an old country rather than what it usually was: the place bustled with early straddlers vying for a seat at the beginning of happy hour for $6.99 martinis and $1.25 oysters and $3.99 dim sum at the bar. The restaurant, like all others, remained half-shuttered and only served takeout.

He later WhatsApp-ed his sister to say that there were now only "morose hours in SF," to which she replied, "America in the gloaming."

What he ordered: Kung Pao chicken, moo shu pork, Mongolian beef, and stir-fried snow peas in garlic sauce.

"Want free soup?" Mrs. Wong asked.

He snorted. She looked at him.

"Free soup's funny?"

"Sorry, Mrs. Wong. No, the soup's too heavy to carry."

After giving his orders, the boy went out and sat on the weathered wooden bench, its green paint flaking off. He watched gentle waves lapping against the shore, felt the sea breeze. He breathed in deeply; it was a reprieve to be outside, away from home.

A few people were strolling up and down the beach. He heard children's laughter. It was hard to process that the country was rolling in the deep, as in shit. It was harder to focus on his homework. Still if only for Leia, he pored over his book, highlighting certain sentences, writing ideas and observations and questions in the margins.

"Discuss the role that class and money play in the relationship of the main characters in LitToC." Or, "Discuss how illness and aging inform romantic love." So went the assignment.

The teacher picked the novel as "it's apropos to our current situation."

"He's a bit of a wooz & a tad sentimental," was his text to Leia. Her curt reply an hour later: "Yup. So JJ, let's just get it done." More like a command than currying for favor, in retrospect.

The thick paperback in his hands under sunlight demanded attention, a worn dog-eared analog that belonged to his sister. But Marquez's Florentino is an immoral a-hole, and Fermina—*su objeto de amoroso*—is an overly pretentious class-climbing bitch. Yet, isn't that the great theme of literature? All, even the decrepit and seriously flawed with one foot in the grave, can be redeemed by love? But tiring, too, he thought, that this *pas de deux* between men and women kept going even when the world goes to shit.

Still, an enjoyable read it was. And later, more so upon rereading.

Who else can get away with phrases like "he dared to explore her withered neck with his fingertips . . . her hips with their decaying bones, her thighs with their aging veins?" Or this kicker of a sentence: "By virtue of marrying a man she does not love for money. That's the lowest kind of whore."

"Huh? Then what of Jan?" he had written on the margin. If she married for love, her rising portfolio saw the end of that. As the world shifted, Stan lost confidence, became diminutive in many ways. Jan, on the other hand, gained and gained. Love was replaced by mutual resentment.

If he had to guess, he would conclude, in the final autopsy, that one can stay together even when love has long faded, one could even tolerate low-grade resentment and apathy, but when there's mutual disrespect, the house will fall. Two cars in the garage, a chicken in the very nice pot, but it ended, like the promises to cherish and love, on the floor.

The OP is where his parents went on their first date when she was an MBA student at San Francisco State and he was teaching a night class there on the art of sales and bargaining. "She was a knockout," Stan used to say, "and a fast learner." "He was a sweet talker," she used to say, not in an unkind way. "I guess he's a good salesman at heart."

It was at the OP that they had their first wedding anniversary, too, and then their tenth, and countless birthday parties in between. But before their eleventh, it all went south, with her discovering of his adultery. There was yelling and screaming and crying, and then a truce. But long before the beer bug bit, they stopped dining in and only did pick-ups. Too many memories to sit through Column A with Peking duck at the OP, their favorite, in a dying marriage.

This bench holds many tender memories, the boy knew. It felt like home. In the living room of their house hangs a photo of Jan sitting next to three-year-old Stacy and JJ as a tiny babe in her arms, smiling to the camera on this bench. She seemed quite happy. So did Stacy. The sun in their eyes. The baby might be giggling as well. He traced his fingers on the worn, flaked-paint bench.

It was then that he heard a familiar laugh. He looked. He recognized her immediately. Leia was walking by with a young man, and they were holding hands. She wasn't wearing a mask. Neither was the young man. Tall and athletic, the guy towered over her, and she leaned into his arm as they walked the beach. Too engaged in conversation, she didn't notice him.

She was barefoot, as if dancing some version of the jig in the way she walked. The young man held her shoes in his other hand and smiled affectionately down at her.

He didn't see Suzanne, the Wong's teenage daughter, until she hovered over him with the big bag for food in hand. "JJ, here you go. I put a couple of extra fortune cookies for your super-funny grandma."

"Thanks."

"She was telling my mother, who was trying to figure out taxes: 'It's not deductible if it's suckable!'"

He could barely see Suzanne's face under her blue mask; the sun was behind her. But her laughter was clear and loud. They didn't talk much at school but acknowledged each other in the hallway.

"Listen, you should order more often. We might not be around much longer."

"What? No shit!"

"Yeah, it's tough keeping this place going. My parents are going crazy not being able to pay for costs. We're losing money. Big time. Two, three more months, maybe. A year? Fuck no. Might shut down by fall if this bug thing keeps going."

Then, looking at her parents working behind the counter through the glass pane, she said in a muffled voice, "I grew up in this damn place. Maybe they'll sell it to a big In-N-Out or something and move to Hawaii."

Then she laughed. "Might be a good thing, though. I like luaus."

He laughed too, thinking of the old couple drinking piña coladas by the pool.

"Okay," he said.

"Bye," she said and went inside. He waved and pretended not to see tears in her eyes.

When he looked again to the beach, the couple had moved further south. His gaze followed them until they were gone from sight. He remained on the old bench, not budging. Far out near horizon, bright cumulus clouds slowly darkened toward amber, toward crimson.

His face felt hot despite the cool air. He took out his iPhone. He dictated into Notes: "I am writing to accept your offer to enroll in the English Department at Yale with a concentration in the creative writing program. Thank you very much. I appreciate your patience and consideration during the admissions process during such difficult times. I look forward to attending your program this fall. And I am excited by the opportunities that await."

The wind grew colder, but he felt heated and flustered. He tried to calm his jumbled thoughts. From time to time, the spicy garlic aroma from the food in the bag next to him wafted upward and permeated the air. And because love and heartbreak and resentment and forgiveness—the messiness of living; the stories yet to be told—were stretching out far beyond sight, his stomach babbled and growled. Still, he kept sitting there, waiting for the people and circling seagulls to turn into silhouettes, a tableau of something that he'd remember as poignant, if bitter-sweet, at twilight.

Swimming from the Mekong Delta

CHICAGO!

How y'all doing?

Keeping warm?

Brrrrrhurrhhh . . . it's so cold, man, how d'y'all live here? I mean, I shared an Uber from O'Hare, and can you believe this: a fat lady had both of her hands in my pants pockets! No, I'm serious here. I didn't even open my mouth to say nothing 'cause she was like, "Don't get any idea, buster. I'm trying to keep warm here."

Now, I wasn't exactly happy with the situation, but either I get off her lap and take my hands out from between her thighs, or shut the fuck up. I mean, a shared ride is a shared ride, right?

Got to keep warm, bro.

Seriously though, for a Vietnamese from Santa Clara, this—this is like landing on the freakin' moon, man.

But cold or not cold, let's just say one thing I learned from being a refugee is that you get used to anything. Compared to my first winter in the good old US o' A when I was yay high, Chicago in January is a walk in the park. I mean, my Mama's still fond of referring to that first winter as: Apocalypse Then.

So, we arrived straight from the Palawan camp in the Philippines, where it was a balmy ninety-five degrees Fahrenheit, and were placed in a refugee camp in Fort Leavenworth on one early February evening, where it was, like, two degrees. When we kids saw snow, we screamed: "wow: it's so beau-ti-ful. It's magic." But a minute after my younger sister, brother, and I ran out of the cabin to play, it was like: Game Over. We learned real fast that when the windchill factor is below zero, snot and body fluids could be used as lethal weapons. I mean, how can you live in a place where you can blind someone with your phlegm? Where murder is as simple as locking the kitchen door after you asked your cheating husband to go out and dump the garbage?

So cold that when we started to learn English, this was how my little bro spelled winter: R-E-G-R-E-T.

Really, the only person I know who can survive this weather? My ex-wife, Michelle!

If there's a blow-out at the Mag Mile in the middle of a cold snap—no problem. Michelle'd put on her mink stove and goggles, grab my credit cards, and ice skate down Michigan Ave at minus twenty. Her idea of an anti-depressant? No, not Prozac, nor Zoloft, nor Paxil, man. No, it's Black Friday.

Friends are fond of calling her Hurricane Michelle. Wet and gusty at the start, but when she's done, she takes away the house, the dog, and the car. Michelle wanted too much of everything. Chanel bags. Jimmy Choo shoes. New face. New body.

And on top of it, a lot of sex!

Now you laugh. Guys, you think guys love sex more than girls, well, you're fucking wrong. That's why God gives them multiple orgasms in exchange for having to give birth. Right? So much so that if you fucked her three times a week, it's still not enough. Men shoot their loads and roll over. Women? They reach orgasm and be like, what, appetizers okay, but where's the entree?

Do Asians have different orgasms than Americans?

Who dat? Oh, hello Mr. Heckler. Of course, we do . . . We cum with subtitles.

Oh, now he laughs, Mr. Heckler—fat guy, front row, on the left here, pissing his pants.

Psst, listen: future comedians, nothing disarms hecklers more than jizz jokes.

But—ahem, back to the story.

So, we spent our first winter in America under siege at Valley Forge. And like George Washington, we too, watched TV. To be more precise,

Brady Bunch reruns. And we dreamed that, someday, we'd be divorced and raise somebody else's kids, and live the American Dream, and with a no-nonsense lesbian named Alice as a maid. Seriously though, that's when it sank into me: I wanted that house, that good life, that pursuit-of-happiness thing.

I grew up in California. I didn't do so well in school, but I got to be a dental assistant right, and made decent wage, but not enough for the lavish lifestyle. Still, got my girl a Porsche. I gave her everything, man. But you know, when you work with teeth day in, day out, and she wants to hump all night long, you just can't. And Michelle's like, "honey, eat me." So I'm down there half asleep, I said, "Michelle, honey, have you started smoking, your gums are swollen." So, you can imagine, it kinda pissed her off.

Michelle herself was bad at giving BJs. She kept using her teeth, and it scraped my dick like fuck. I mean, I couldn't complain 'cause, like, getting a BJ from Michelle happens as often as when we have Daylight Savings Time, either that or it's when she's lobbying for the latest Gucci purse. So you grin and you bear it. I mean, what's a little scraping and bleeding? I'd tell myself, it's just like teeth cleaning. Grin and bear it. You're about to blast a $5,000 wad and gain an extra hour.

Of course, I did tell Tom, my boss at the dental office, about the oral problem, and he felt sorry for me. He was sympathetic.

So much so that when I came home one day early from a sterilization and disinfection conference in Vegas, I found Michelle giving Tom a BJ in my living room. She was licking his nuts too, while he was messing with her hair. Michelle'd never let me touch her hair, mind you, and she never sucked my balls. She said she hated looking at wrinkles.

And here's Tom, my boss, in the living room, with his pants down: "Now, now, Kevin, it is not what you think. I just, you know, uhm, felt bad about the scrapings, so I brought over some high-end night guards, and next thing you know, Michelle wanted to test them out. You'll be okay now. Buddy, as an added bonus, Michelle won't grind her teeth in the middle of the night and wake you up anymore."

You've got to admit, in his own ways, Tom was kinda thoughtful.

But honestly? She was sucking nuts, man! His nuts! That's so extra. Hell, the only tea-bagging I ever did was being too proud to accept Obamacare after I lost my job for removing Tom's two front teeth.

Oh my god, three people got that joke. And they all sit on the far right.

That was how we broke up—and how my *Brady Bunch* dream fell apart. And how I started doing standup. My little stint in prison taught me I can entertain the lifers. Because here's a secret: if you can make them laugh, they most likely won't beat you up, or make you their bitch, 'cause they can't keep a hard-on.

Dudes, people change, okay. People betray. My dream turned to shit. Michelle was all sweet when we first met as FOBs in high school, but she went all Material Girl soon after we married. She was My-Linh in high school, but by the time she got to college, My-Linh became Michelle, and she refused to speak a word of Vietnamese 'cause she's somehow, hm like, oh my gawd, forgotten it? She's a middle child. Need I say more? She's Jan Brady Nguyen, not getting the love.

Hell, my ex rewrote her bio in one swoop. This is how she talked about her coming over here from Vietnam to her best friend in college. This is Michelle: "No, no, no, we did not come by boat. Darling, we flew. The worst thing that happened was, when I reached for the champagne, the stewardess slapped my hand. I was not of drinking age. Slapped my hand? Bitch, why the hell did you put bubbly on the tray with the Coke and Pepsi in front of me? I mean, I'd been drinking this stuff as a child back in Saigon on special occasions. Girl, I was traumatized for years."

And I was like: Who are you? And what have you done to my girlfriend?

News flash: Michelle was a boat person just like me, but she pretended that she was never poor, never homeless. Instead of living in a small house at the edge of the city, her house in the recalling was a grand villa in the center of Saigon with servants and a French-speaking chauffeur. Her dad, who was a sergeant in the army, was posthumously upgraded to a colonel.

Why the fuck does everyone inflate their story when they come to America? I mean, fuck, if I had a dollar for every Vietnamese I met in California who claimed to be on the last helicopter out of Vietnam, I would have 10,000 bucks! How the hell do you know yours was the last? Would it kill you if it was the second to the last? It's a helicopter, bitches, not an air-fucking-craft carrier, okay?

• • • •

So, guess what is big in the Little Saigons? The Biggest Thing. Here, I'll give you a clue. Look at this in my hand: that's right—a credit card. No, not getting into gambling debt, you cynics, that's the second biggest thing.

No: it's plastic. As in plastic surgery.

Hear ye, hear ye, my rap of woe:

> *Uh, Uh,*
> *My girl was self-effacin'*
> *till she discovered laser resurfacin'*
> *we were so happy, 'til she found rhinoplasty,*
> *(and me an accessory)*
> *Uh*
> *She once lacked pretension,*
> *Then Homegirl got hooked on*
> *micro-dermabrasion*
> *Used to kiss me now all she does is dis me*
> *Used to give me honey when I made da money*
> *Out of cash?*
> *Homegirl made a dash*
> *Uh, Uh, Uh,*
> *Neck Lift, Brow Lift, Breast lift,*
> *Made me a working stiff*
> *Liposuction and Tummy Tuck; she's so plastic pretty now*
> *that our love was . . . out-a luck.*

Thank you. Thank you so very much . . . for applauding my tragedy.
Thanks a lot.

Seriously though: don't tell anybody this, 'cause it's kinda, like, a secret, okay: shh! Yes, we escaped from the commies, risked death and starvation and got marooned on isolated islands eating dirt and tree bark, risked getting kidnapped and sold into slavery in Thailand or Malaysia, all this, for what? Yup, to finally look pretty in America.

High cheekbones, slim waist, and tan. Funny how we were so skinny and sunburned on that boat out at sea, but in America, we spend a fortune just to look that way again.

Botox. Liposuction. Double eyelids. Aquiline nose. Chemical peels. Micro-needling. Split chins. You name it, man!

Now you would think that a country that defeated the French, and then the US, would find Western features fugly after seeing John Wayne shoot our people. But you'd be, like, WRONG. Vietnamese put down those Amerasian kids right, 'cause they say "these kids are all children of whores, fathered by American GIs." The kids were treated like dirt back in Nam. But don't tell nobody, okay: it's between us: many of us want to look exactly like them. You know, light hair, blue or hazel eyes, straight nose, double eyelids, split chins, the works.

You open a newspaper or magazine in Little Saigon and what'd you see? Ads? Ads for nasty shit like "tattoo your nipple to make it pinker!" "Pluck your eyebrows and tattoo in perfect ones!" "Dimples, buy one, get one free."

For a split chin, there's acid injections to eat the flesh, and to have a dimple, an awl through your cheeks, so simple. I mean, why pluck out your eyebrow and put in permanent ink makeup? It's like having a colonic and then, I don't know, stuffing yellow and brown crayons up your ass.

My thinking on beauty? It's all pain.

Waterboarding? Pshaw. You think binding feet is easier? They break the bones and reset them to make you walk funny. Or those big ass clay discs in those tribal women's lips in Africa. Stretch and stretch and stretch until your lips can carry dinnerware. Comes in mighty handy at a picnic. And you don't even want to know what the men needed to stretch to fit the silverware.

Methinks Homeland Security would do better extracting info from potential terrorists if it threatened them with plastic surgery. "No, please, please don't make me beautiful!" "Oh no, please, I'll tell you where Al-Qaeda's hiding. Please, not another liposuction! I can't. Please, no, not the split chin and rhinoplasty and laser resurfacing treatment. I'll tell. I'll tell."

I mean, can you imagine Guantanamo Bay prisoners who resisted talking all ending up looking like runway models by the time HS's done with them? All gaunt, dimpled smiles, and high cheekbones, with smooth acid-washed skin? And if you want to practice cruel and unusual punishment? Give them full collagen-injected lips, buttock augmentation, turn them into pretty boys with bubble butts. It'll be really fun to come home to Yemen and Saudi Arabia with them lips. Imagine having to share bunk beds with all those bearded dudes so hard up they're willing to blow themselves up just for a shot at having sex with some virgins in heaven.

I was at this wedding in Orange County last month, right. It was a modest Vietnamese wedding, which means somewhere between 300 to 500 guests. Every weekend, the same thing: half of Little Saigon showed up and the other half bitching about not being invited. Thing is, with all the new money, people are still so damn lazy. They all be going to the same fucking cosmetic surgeon and same handful of dressmakers for traditional dresses. So they all got the same nose, same double eyelids, and the same fucking traditional dress with different types of flowers sewn on them.

Now at these weddings, there's a bottle of Courvoisier in the middle that gets replenished when it's empty. After a few shots, and after spinning that damn Lazy Susan so many times, it's like it's not just the tray that spins, know what I mean? Guys start tripping. Oh god, which one is my wife, man, and which one's yours?

Lazy Susan, by the way, is a weird name to call a revolving tray on a table. Who the hell came up with that? I've been racking my brain about this: and my only educated guess is that the inventor named it to get back at his ex-wife, Suzy.

So hey, here's a cool idea for a new genre in porn: lazy porn! "Dallas does Lazy Susan." Why? 'Cause Susan's too lazy to do Dallas. It'll be surreal. Lazy Susan's so lazy she's just gonna lie there, and every cowboy spins and screws her while she eats her dim sum. Lazy Susan's so lazy that after a giving few blow jobs, she'd be applying for unemployment benefits. Lazy Susan's so lazy that she'd outsource all her hand jobs to India.

• • • •

Used to kiss me now all she does is dis me
Used to give me honey when I made da money . . .

You know the first English sentence I learned before coming to America?

"No money, no honey."

The second one is "Me love you long time."

I heard it spoken by prostitutes in Saigon during the war. Which made me kind of Miss Saigon's raunchier little bro, Lolito Nguyen serving that special 10 percent of American GI's population on R&R.

But can you imagine going to seventh grade in Colma, Daly City, the only suburb of San Francisco, talking like that? A bunch of tough working-class neighborhood kids surrounding you and asking all kind of questions? Are you a Viet Cong? Did you kill GIs? Are you a spy?

And the only thing you could say the first few weeks was "Me love you long time"?

And "No money, no honey"? It gets your ass kicked, or in my case, turned on my racist, and pedarastic, math teacher, baldy Mr. O'Brien.

One day, he kept me after school and pulled down his zipper and called me over like he was trying to feed a barnyard chicken: "Sucky, fucky, come here. Sucky fucky." He even called me "little boat peepee." So I came over, licked my lips, then swiftly kicked him in the nuts, so hard that fucker bent over and saw imaginary numbers. "So sucky to be you, Mr. O'Brien."

So I learned English. Fast. I memorized commercials like a parrot.

Soon, my mother'd be looking at me like was possessed by the devil. But man, I just didn't want to get beat up at school because of my accent or my lack of English. I just swallowed English sentences whole to fit in.

I mean, I went from this kid who spoke Vietnamese in the sweetest voice to this craggy-throaty teenager who spoke broken English. And it literally shattered my vocal cords. And it changed me inside out. Things were happening everywhere, not just my throat. I mean, especially down there. I was getting all these weird tingling feelings, and I would get so hard in the morning. And I thought, "English's magic. I can't stop speaking it. And it made my dick hard."

It was like my penis wanted to speak English, too.

I mean, no one in my family said nothing about the birds and the bees, and definitely not about the honey. So thank god for my homie, Marvin Randez. He and I consulted the seventh grade Bible, a very reliable source for information, with useful graphics and detail studies of this "honey money" phenomenon. It's called *Hustler* magazine—which Marvin mooched from his dad. That's right, the Leviticus chapter. We hid a few under his desk and pored over its pure, hard data during lunch, and he said this was what's happening and this is what also is happening when you do this.

I was left in no uncertain terms to discover how to make my own honey, so to speak, often in the shower when the showerhead kept spraying on my woody. It got me feeling so good that I was, hands down, the cleanest kid on the block. Always showering and shampooing and shit.

My bologna has a new name, too. It's Cabo, after Henry Cabot

Lodge, who was some senator in early twentieth century. Swear to you, true story. We were studying US history in seventh grade and Marvin, tripping on being my teacher and all, leaned over and said, "We all name our penis at a certain age in America. Mine is Martin Luther King Jr. Joe behind you named his Louis the 14th, as in fourteen inches. Hahaha. And my dad, he's really big, so it's Jose Escudero de Paula Juan Nepomuceno de Arroyo Martínez."

Then he said, "So to be American, you need to name yours, too. It's like a coming-of-age thing."

I was like, What? Okay. Cool. But, I mean, I didn't know what name to pick. So Marvin picked Henry Cabot Lodge "'cause he's important or something." Then he added, "but considering your size, let's just call it Cab for now."

Man, talk about cold, Chicago. But having thus christened him, Cab and I went home and promptly named the showerhead Cindy, you know, after Cindy Crawford. "Cindy, good to see you again!" "Yeah, Cindy, you gonna spray Cab real good? Hard? Make Cab real clean? Okay?" Whenever the water pressure was full and hot, Cindy would deliver. Oh yeah. Then Cab, let me tell you, ain't just Cab anymore. He's like "right now, my name is Henry! Cabot! Lodge!"

"Spray Cabot right there, Cindy, oh, God, hmm, Cindy, Cindy, Cindy!" But all too soon, my eyes would roll to the back of my head, and my knees would buckle, and it was like I was on the verge of fainting.

"Damn, Cindy, Cab's all dirty again!"

After a while, it got so bad that my family complained: "Why are you so clean all of sudden?"

Does Cabot have an accent?

Does Cab have an accent? asks Mr. Front Row Heckler. He's back, ladies and gentlemen! Yeah, sure, it's from Bridgeport. Every morning, it sez: "For cryin' out loud! Where Cindy at? She's so hat." Or, "What da fuck. Why chew keeping beating me four?"

Does Cabot have an accent! Seriously, why people be so discriminating?

The other day, I was doing my set, and this old guy started yelling: "Go Home, Chinaman!" Folks, I think that old man mistook the headline "Swimming from the Mekong Delta" outside for an anti-immigrant rally. Go home? Dear Mr. Sauerkraut: for years, Uncle Sam reaches under Miss Saigon's skirt for some honey and you tell me to go home? Uncle Sam played with her titties, bombed her secret trails, and left agent orange in her garden; hell, he pounded her so hard that's how I got here, to you, onstage, telling you stories. News flash: if you cum on Asia, Asia comes to you.

Seriously. We worked hard, man. We chased the Dream like it's a lifesaver. This is why I'm up here, working night after night. You think it's easy, then Mr. Heckler, you waddle up these here steps, and tell a joke every twenty seconds to make what, a couple, a few, couple measly million bucks a year? After tax?

Now, everybody, clap if you love Chinese food . . .

Aaaand . . . the only dude in the front row who didn't clap, ladies and gentlemen, is Asian. Dude, who the fuck is Asian, lives in Chicago, and never had Chinese? What are you, North Korean? Or were you adopted by the Amish and snuck out during Rumspringa? Get your Princess Leia buns earmuffs ready. I'm taking you to extra spicy Szechuan after the show.

Okay, now clap if you or your loved ones had their ass wiped by a Filipino nurse in a hospital . . . okay, now ladies, and some of you gentlemen, too, clap if you have your nails done by a Vietnamese? Okay. Wow. That's crazy. Mr. Heckler, thanks for clapping. I must say: love your well-manicured hands.

My Ma? Her first job in America was sewing in a small factory. One of the things she sewed were American flags and Klansmen costumes, okay. But the KKKs complained. She made the slits for eyes too small and almond-shaped. And it confused the Klansmen so much, 'cause they started to beat up on each other and told each other to go back to Asia.

Seriously, Americans. You ask us to cook your food, wipe your ass, do your nails, clean your house, babysit your kids, cut your grass, pick your grapes, and then you keep telling us that we need to go home? Makes me wonder, how do you expect us to multitask all the time?

I have a racist friend, right, his name is Danny. But let's just call him, I don't know, asshole? He's an Amerasian from Vietnam who hated Mexicans and Blacks. Go figure. And his favorite food? Tacos and burritos. He said the only reason he wouldn't move to Oregon to join the Aryan community is because Nazi food's so bland. He would miss Mexican food too much. Sometimes the asshole would show up in the drive-thru at Taco Bell and order a three crunchy tacos combo and the entire staff to go build the wall.

He also looked down on Vietnamese, too. So I said to him, I said, asshole, you know what your problem is. You don't love yourself. You wish to cut out the other half if you could. So here's a knife. Try it. If you can cut out your contradiction, you're the man. So Danny just broke down and cried. He said nobody loved him. Not his GI daddy, whom he never met. Not his mommy, the whore who abandoned him.

It made me think. In the end, it's all about love, isn't it? What we do, don't do, should have done, could've or would've, has to do with love.

Love—not loved enough. Loved too much. Never loved. Longing for it. Got rejected from it. Running from it. Doing crazy thing because of it, hoping it would come to you, or stay with you. Even escaping out to sea to possibly die with your kids—it's crazy, but it's also 'cause you love your children so much that you'd rather risk them dying looking to be free than to live oppressed.

Our relationship with this thing called love sets our paths in life.

Me, for instance. I thought life was straightforward. You marry your high school sweetheart and go to work cleaning teeth and have a family. I was not smart like my siblings, but I was all about being a dental assistant and making the mortgage and paying for that red Porsche. All that time slaving away, my boss was giving my wife more than fillings and floss.

It goes to show: Life can throw you a curveball when you expect a slider, a screwball when you expect a splitter. Whatever vision you have of your future, let me tell you—it most likely won't turn out the way you expect it. Try to fulfill someone else's material desires as your own happiness—isn't it about trying to fill the void in your heart? And clearly wasn't my ex trying to fill that void in hers with them purses and plastic surgery?

"No money, no honey!"
  "Me love you long time!"
  Funny, those two phrases were the only English I knew when I got here, and it took me a long time to realize real honey can never be bought with money. And how you gonna love anybody long time when you don't even like yourself short time?
  Funnier how heartbreak can lead to a new vocation. I mean, I went to anger management as part of the judge's sentencing and the more I told my stories, the more the guys cracked up. Slowly, I realized that I was funny, funny enough to make rapists and murderers and my therapist teary-eyed from laughter. And funny enough to make someone way beyond my league fall for me.
  Yes, yes, I am dating now. A professor in anthropology from Berkeley. But I take it slow. S.L.O.W.
  I won't go into details, but she's a vegetarian, with a special diet with an emphasis on nuts. I'm learning to love but not rush into things. Again, I won't go into details, but she says I deserve the Henry Cabot Lodge sobriquet. So far, we're doing alright. I think I am a special subgroup for her new ethnography: boat people who became comedians.

And you know what? I ran into Michelle last year after I was doing this little gig in San Diego. She didn't seem surprised to see me. Or maybe she was, I mean, how can you tell with all that Botox? With her arched eyebrows, her new silicone-injected lips, she seemed to be in this perpetual state of being amused. It's eerie, 'cause she never liked any of my jokes.
  Anyway, she was like, "Hey, Kevin!" and I was like, "Oh, shit! Ah hi—hi, Michelle."

She was in this tight green sequined minidress. You can tell she wanted to hook up again, the way she tossed her hair over her shoulder, and full of compliments on my success. And she was dropping subtle hints like saying, "Kevin, maybe we should hook up again."

And if that's not subtle enough, she added: "With these new lips I'll blow you out of the water."

But there's no vibe there, you know what I mean. Them lips looked like they've been vulcanized for a long cross-country road trip. I wasn't giving her the cold shoulder, exactly. But I was busy hugging myself in the middle of palmy San Diego, 'cause I felt cold all over, like chills running up and down my spine, like when you entered the *Brady Bunch* house and then realized it's an empty set, and there's this inner voice that whispers: "Yo! Hold on to your wallet! And run!"

After a couple minutes, Michelle gave up.

"Okay, whatever, Kevin, just don't talk so much about all the plastic stuff, okay?" she said.

I was like, "Oh . . . kay . . . bye Michelle."

So, I watched in wonder as she wandered away and faded like a shimmering green beacon into the dark. Out in the ocean, there were a bunch of boats, and they were lit up. It was so beautiful. And I thought: how many years was I obsessed with this person, but who now looks like she could melt if she got too close to a torch light? I felt like hugging her then. But already she was gone, borne back ceaselessly into the past.

By the way, Michelle, yo! If you're watching this on YouTube or Instagram or whatever, 'cause homies here in the front row are filming me, illegally: #mybad. I realized now what was between us is nothing more than an illusion. But feel free to click on that thumbs-up button if you like.

I lost the house, the job, the car, and my American Dream went up in smoke. I was almost made muscle-bound DeAndre Washington's bitch in the slammer.

But thanks to you, Michelle, ma belle, I also found something important: material.

No honey, no money? No worries.
Baby, I found my tongue. I found my way in the world.
Okay. That's it. That's my set. Thank you! Thank you!
Keep warm, CHICAGO!
PEACE OUT!

What We Talk About When We Can't Talk About Love

Friends call him BP, short for Boat People—purposefully plural for his autobiography of seemingly multiple personalities. At various gatherings, and after a few drinks, one story or another of BP's Great Escape was shared; sometimes two or three versions were told, one right after the other, to hilarious effect. The name became something of a running joke.

There was one in which he, in the dark of night, rowed out in a floating basket and snuck onto a fishing boat rumored to be carrying fleeing refugees and became a teenage stowaway. Another version tells of his ethnic Chinese-Vietnamese parents from Saigon's Chợ Lớn district, who—after the capital fell to the Communist Army, the currency turned worthless, and they starved—sent him on a one-way ticket out to sea.

Yet in another version, there is no family—he's an orphan runaway from an abusive factory owner who used him for more than mere labor, including selling Boat People's services to his friends.

But it had been a rice cake factory, he recalled with a toothy grin. "Abused? Yes. But so was the entire country. Besides, Boat People were eating."

Or he was the son of a Chinese tycoon living in Saigon, tasked with helping his father move their gold out of the country after the war ended. In this version, the boat that his father owned sank off the coast of Malaysia. The gold, along with his father and the rest of his family, disappeared into the black abyss.

"It was like *Life of Pi*, but without the tiger," he said.

Then, one night at a cocktail party he hosted to celebrate a friend's job promotion, he told the story of a distant father who lost his fortune when the Vietnamese communists confiscated his rice distribution business, but who nevertheless managed to purchase a seat for his only son on a crowded boat with a combination of his remaining two ounces of gold—the going fare was six—and the promise of his son's indentured servitude.

BP ended up working alongside fishermen in a small village near Vũng Tàu. He learned to fish, but also how to secretly build a bigger boat out of a smaller one. A second tier meant extra room, extra gold from paying passengers.

As apprentice and servant, BP was assigned the task of cooking—which was new to him—and assisting in the boatbuilding. The cooking proved difficult. There were dry leaves and kindling along the riverbank, but when you're thirteen and given only one big pot and nothing else, cooking for ten or more workers was not easy. Often, the fire raged out of control, then died because of the unpredictable wind. He burnt the rice a few times, or else cooked the rice unevenly, and each time, he was beaten by the captain, who once choked him until he passed out.

"He took me up on the unfinished boat and had his way with me," he now said to gasps and whispers of his guests who sat on his veranda overlooking the bay. Something in his voice caused the laughter to die, the smiles to fade. Some stared at him, some at their drinks, some at each other, aghast.

"And the weird thing was," he said in an unusually even tone, "I thought I deserved it. After all, I must have been a bad person, a child abandoned."

An awkward stillness was in the air; jazz music played softly on the Bluetooth speakers. His friends regarded the bridges on the bay from BP's veranda and murmured among themselves. BP busted out laughing.

"Suckers! You really believed it, didn't you? Hahaha!"

But no one laughed.

A handsome young man, new to the group, had tears in his eyes. He too had left Vietnam on a rickety boat, though he hadn't remembered much (he was only three). But he did recall losing a sister on it.

"My mom went through some tough times," he said. "She still does."

BP's best friend, a doctor from Beijing, known among the group as DD, or Dear Doctor for being genuinely kind, stared at BP, dumbfounded.

"I can't believe you went through all that," he managed to say, his face hardly veiling the pain. "I mean, I know you for almost ten years, and that was as real as it's ever gotten. The details . . ."

"It's like the other versions all pale in comparison to this one," another friend, a journalist, agreed. "BP, I know you like making things up. And honestly, I don't know if we'll ever get to the real story, but it was real enough. Of all the ones you told, it was the saddest."

"Very sad," murmured the chorus.

"I hope for your sake that it was invented," said BP's youngest friend. "Call me when you want to talk."

BP backpedaled. "Listen, guys, you know it's for fun, right? You may not believe it, but I am really, honestly, genuinely, absolutely, happy with my life. The past is the past."

"But aren't you curious about how your family's doing?"

"Yeah, BP, don't you want to put the past to rest? Reach out to them, man."

Sober now, and sensing a deflating mood among the group, BP said, "Listen. I am with my family right now. You're all my family. And you all know I like to make up stories to entertain you bitches. Okay, honestly, you're knocking on the wrong door."

Whispers

"What do you make of BP? He's so damn strange."

"It's so sad. He couldn't even talk about what really happened. The trauma . . . so deep."

"Give him time. After what he went through, what he did, he doesn't have to answer to anybody."

"How he lives his life now is a testimony to his strength."

"Heck, we don't even know his real name. It's definitely not BP, nor Robert Chung. Bitch changed everything when he applied for sponsorship to America."

This much was consistent: never once did he contact his family back home, and in each story, there was always a plastic bottle.

And he, after years of struggle, prospered in America.

Among friends, he was often funny, irreverent, the Life of the Party. Among lovers, he was generous.

But otherwise, he was impenetrable, a fortress, an uncrackable wall.

"Don't you think he's always so hyper-alert? That's totally PTSD."

"You're right. But let him be. Who are we to judge? Who among us doesn't have something to hide?"

"He's aggravatingly happy. I mean, can you be satisfied all the time? Can you, like, grow if you claim to have somehow achieved supreme happiness?"

Weekends and Habits

He gave a slightly used, blue Gran Coupe Convertible BMW to a Latino boyfriend in Sacramento, whom he saw on the weekends. They would drive it around town and eat at the finest restaurants. A few expensive cell phones for his frequent lovers, dinner parties for friends on their birthdays, spontaneous trips to Puerto Vallarta, where he owned a condo, for long weekends with his best friend, DD.

"My life is free. Free as a bird. Perfectly happy."

He saw *Othello* once and found the Moor aggravating.

"Why the need to know? Make peace with yourself. Your wife, maybe she screws around, maybe not. Maybe you screw around. So what?" he asked his weekend boyfriend rhetorically. "I'm satisfied to be here. With you. Looking into your eyes. They're beautiful. Isn't that enough?"

The way he said beautiful, it made Weekend Boyfriend believe.

"This moment here, it's always perfect."

For all he knew, he might be quoting the Dalai Lama. It sounded good.

BP has an annoying habit of texting his friends images of what he just bought. A house. A car. A new laptop. A motorcycle. A painting. Half a case of vintage Dom Pérignon. A new entertainment system. Always bought at a discount, a bargain, from the artist himself (bypassing the gallery), from a going-out-of-business store, from a wealthy neighbor, from personal connections. The king of the deal, always so happy with his new toys. His happiness self-evident in JPEG.

BP once went to a Buddhist retreat in Marin County with a friend who told him he had an out-of-body experience after years of deep meditation. This did not surprise BP. He volunteered that he did too, when he was young. "When you are raped repeatedly, you learn to have out-of-body experiences as a defense. You learn to look down at your body and say to yourself: 'That's someone else, not me.'"

The friend stared at him. "You fucking with me, BP?"

"No. I'm totally serious." Then he gave into a fit of giggles.

Survival Skills and Wisdom

But the lessons of the Great Escape continued to inform him. The smallest of things can be a lifesaver, he would instruct his friends and coworkers. "The plastic bottle we throw away everyday can be a lifesaver, to carry water and use as a flotation device."

To get drinking water, he had to wade through the water from the small barren island, which he called Left Nut, where he was allowed to camp, to the larger island nearby, the Right Nut. Though, when it was high tide, it was not a wade but a swim. "So fill your bottle to one third," he would say to his listeners, as if they were stuck in the camp with him. "And with the cap tightly sealed, it's both a water container plus a buoy to help you to get back to your island."

A testament to his survival skills: he spoke Cantonese to the storeowner who was Chinese-Malaysian and managed to serve as a go-between for the boat people living on the poorer island, the Left Nut, and the store outpost located in a fishing village on the Right Nut.

Refugees carried gold and dollar bills and jewelry—all of it traded for extra rations, toothpaste, medicine, or even a transistor radio.

Eventually, he moved from Left Nut to Right—from a small tent under a dead coconut tree to the storage room in the grocery store to guard the owner's rice and other products.

"BP always sleeps where the food is," he would remember fondly.

Indeed, by the time he was given sponsorship to America, he'd amassed a small fortune—$1,127 and a portable radio. For a teenager who had paddled to that promising shore with nothing but a plastic bottle, it was an astounding feat.

What followed were several bad winters in Chicago living with distant relatives who welcomed him with food deprivation, neglect, and verbal abuse, until he got a scholarship to Northwestern, where he promptly discovered his own homosexuality and perfected his knack for making money.

Now a day trader and an IT manager working for a Fortune 500 company offering stock options, he flips houses on the side. Owner of five homes and three sports cars, his pride and joy is the house in the Oakland Hills, overlooking the bay with an unhindered view of all the bridges and San Francisco's fabled downtown high rises that sparkled on clear nights like fairytale castles in the distance.

Why Go Back?

Dear Doctor had the most reliable recon: a weak moment from BP when they were driving to Santa Cruz one late afternoon.

Unexpectedly revealed was the fact that BP was the child of a second wife who suffered from mental illness and had been neglected by his philandering father. In turn, she neglected BP. He was not, therefore, bound by filial duty and obligation. There are other half-siblings, none of whom he really knew. He was just glad to have made it to America and prospered. Nobody cared about him, so why go back? End of story.

"I ain't got a family," BP told DD, who loved his own parents. "It's a blessing."

On rare occasions, however, he would give in to nostalgia.

"Chợ Lớn's chicken rice was the best. There was this restaurant called Cơm Gà Xiu Xiu just a few blocks from my house. My God, some evenings you had to wait an hour. It was divine, though. Man oh man, that old man could cook!"

"Full Moon Festival. My God, how many lanterns did I burn as a child."

Other times, the king of one-liners was flippant.

"Will you ever go home, BP?"

"BP is at home in the world."

"Where's home for you?"

"Home is where my midnight blue Porsche Targa 4S is."

"Why are there so many versions of your life?"

"BP is large. BP contains multitudes. BP sings the booty electric."

"You ever plan to go back there for a visit someday?"

"There's no there there."

"Aren't you curious about your old home?"

"Honey, home isn't where you're from—home is where your mortgage is."

"Why go back, indeed?" he'd ask rhetorically when someone suggested it would help put an end to the obvious sadness. Of his family, there's little to be said.

"I can't believe you have no trauma from what you went through, BP."

"No trauma. No fear. No phobia. The only trauma BP got is from the audit in 2008 from the IRS. BP is so deadly afraid of taxation without representation."

The Fire Next Time

To prove that the past didn't have a hold on him, BP started taking sailing lessons with Dear Doctor, whose job it was also to bear witness to BP's healthy state of mind. The first two lessons went well, but during the third, on an extra windy day in September, the water was choppy. The newbies struggled. The temperature was dropping.

The captain of the *Fair Sark* decided to rely on the boat's engine to get them back in, but first it needed his attention. BP, tired and sunburned, stood at the bow with DD, who brought a small pair of binoculars so they could find BP's house on the hills.

He was about to point out his house when there was a loud bang, followed by several screams. The captain, who was fixing the engine, had an astonished look on his face as he stared at his own arm: it was on fire, and so was the engine.

A blur of motion: the fire extinguisher was employed, the doctor went to attend to the captain's burns, someone radioed for help, people made unconscious and conscious adjustments to their life vests.

The boat continued to rock. The waves were pounding against the bow like determined battering rams. Things eventually calmed, but after a few minutes, smoke spilled out from somewhere deep inside the ship's bowels; a hidden fire and the one extinguisher all spent.

"Should we jump, BP?" DD asked, trying to sound calm. He trusted BP's instincts more than his own. Given the amount of smoke, he sensed a fire could erupt very soon. People stood upwind ready to jump, causing the ship to list badly. But BP hadn't moved from his spot at the bow. He was still holding onto the binoculars, trying to keep his balance.

"No, DD, not yet," he said, without averting his gaze of the hills. "Let's wait. Water's too cold right now to last long in it. Stand as far from the engine as you can. And watch out for other boats."

Bobbing and rocking above the water, he stood steadily, transfixed by his house, which he'd never seen from this angle before. The sliding glass doors facing the bay shimmered yellow-red as if they, too, were on fire. Odd how, before sunset, everything took on an extra glow, a light exquisite. The hills dotted with beautiful homes seemed to him like some unknown kingdom at dusk.

Part of him made mental calculations. Other boats must certainly have spotted the billowing smoke and would surely come to the rescue. Too bad so many seemed so far away, with the smoke less visible at sunset. The Coast Guard was no doubt on the way.

If he were to jump, his iPhone would need to be secured in the sandwich bag, which he had kept after lunch. He took it out now and quickly ate a few baby carrots to keep his energy up, giving the rest to DD. He put the cell phone in the now empty bag and zipped it up. He took off his shoes and belt as they would add weight in the water. The current drifted southwest, which meant he, with his life jacket, should swim to the closest shore at a thirty- to thirty-five-degree angle. It should send him near those restaurants that had neon lights blinking near Hunter's Point, something clear to aim for in the dark. But it would be toward the opposite side of the East Bay, far from home, an inconvenience. And it would be dark, and he'd be hard to find in the water if the current took him off track, not to mention possibly getting killed by one of those freight ships.

He almost laughed at the irony: to drown in the temperate Bay when the tempestuous ocean couldn't kill him. He saw himself. Dead. Floating face down in the water. Drifting with the tide while the house, its porch lights beckoning, faded farther and farther away.

Was he afraid of dying?

No. Not really.

His calculations were on point, and the risks at the moment were minimal.

Chances were good. Help was coming. The Coast Guard would be, at most, thirty minutes from arriving. He would wait for the last minute to minimize hypothermia. He had a big voice. The cell phone—now ensconced in the sandwich bag, its battery three-quarters full—would be a bright light if he used his flash app intermittently.

Yet it was something else—a nagging feeling—that made him breathless. He didn't want to give it clarity. But there it was: an extra weight, an unreasonable fear that nevertheless was tugging at him.

"BP, fire's getting worse," DD said. He touched BP's shoulder. "I don't know—maybe we should jump?"

Behind them, a few more people leapt into the water to join half of the crew, all floating about the boat, bitching about the cold and trying to form a circle.

BP hugged DD. Even in this wind, he could still smell the briny odor of dry scallops on DD's sweater—DD's mother, who lives with him, cooks it on occasion, and it clings to all of the doctor's clothing.

BP closed his eyes. Suddenly, a vision of another kitchen came back: a woman bending over a wok, the coal burning steadily inside a clay oven. He saw a little boy on a tricycle peddling in circles on the kitchen floor. He heard laughter, the clanging of dishes.

"No. Not yet!" he yelled into DD's ear. "We should wait, stand here, enjoy the view!"

The boat kept rocking. He focused on keeping his balance. Everyone's shadows danced and elongated across the shimmering, darkening waters around the hull.

"BP, aren't you scared?"

"Not at all!"

What he couldn't tell anybody, even in his many drunken versions of his Great Escape, and what he had nearly forgotten until now, was that when he jumped from that crowded boat, he nearly drowned. Nearly two weeks of barely eating and drinking and little movement had severely weakened him, and his muscles had atrophied. Though the two islands didn't appear that far away—the nearest perhaps two hundred meters at most—it was a daunting distance with the waves and opposing current.

The skinny teenager sank.

Seawater got into his eyes, his nose. Terror took over. About him, bodies slipped one by one into the sea. A watery grave. He screamed. What bubbled out of his mouth were resentments and a curse against fate—how he hated his hunger, his smallness, his helplessness; how he wanted to stab that rapist in the eye. Yet screaming only made him sink lower, and the golden surface of the water turned into an impossible sky.

Did time stop then? In his recalling, that moment between deciding to swallow seawater and drown, or to struggle and survive, was an eternity. A slowness to everything. And a deep silence. His life ran backward—an unhappy childhood, a crazed mother, a philandering father—and the tenderness too: that new school uniform his father bought him at the An Đông market, the way his mother combed his hair gently and slowly after a shower, readying him for school. That was before things went badly, and the abuse and neglect began. The sadness and joy, all the pains, somehow seeped out of his tiny body as if black ink into the sea.

He heard his own mumbled scream then. The clock ticked. A surge of something inside, and it felt almost like joy. The half-inflated water bottle, which he clutched unconsciously, had apparently decided for him, buoying him upward, toward life. He instinctively kicked and kicked. Now retching and coughing, he found his bearing. His eyes burning from seawater, he paddled toward the blurry shore.

Now standing on another listing boat, years later, he marveled at the strength and swiftness with which he'd saved himself. But was it someone else who broke the surface, swallowing seawater on the way up, and thrashed about gasping for air?

The Other Boy

And now the sea glistened, turning velvety with the night.

"I think we should jump. We can even make it to shore from here, yes? The captain said everyone should when there's fire," said DD. A few splashes sounded from the back of the boat. Someone was cussing loudly in the frigid water.

But BP chuckled.

"To jump or not to jump? That is the egression."

"What?"

"Doctor Dear, what if the other boy didn't drown?"

DD stared at his friend. "Robert Chung, what do you mean?"

BP ignored him and spontaneously composed a poem in Chinese:

Hidden barnacled hands, wanting
Life above the waves
Boy's screams bubble into foam
Naked and cold he

Be reaching this distant shore yet

His house gleamed and sparkled, a golden beacon high upon the hills. Out of the corner of his eye, he saw DD struggling to take off his sneakers and socks. In an orderly manner, he arranged his socks inside the shoes and lined them neatly next to his backpack as if he were coming home to his sparklingly clean condo.

Fire erupted under a deep purple dome of a sky.

A few more splashes sounded. In the water, the crew bobbed and jounced.

The moment before jumping: the dryness of his tongue, the quivering of his lips, the cold of the wind against his fingers. He swallowed hard, heard his saliva go down his throat, felt his heart beat against his chest. Everything was beautiful, even the billowing smoke. He looked for the house again, but it had long faded from view, hiding among the shadows.

"DD, here's a riddle," he whispered just before his friend leaped.

"I mean, can't we both?"

5A, 5B, DEST: SGN

He touched her, barely a tap on the arm, and startled her. She turned from her window. So absorbed with the golden surface of the sea below she hadn't heard the flight attendant's solicitation.

"Ma'am, some more champagne?"

"Ah! So sorry. Please. A little more."

They were flying business class, each secured in their own world. Passengers were listening to music, or working on their laptops, or reading, and the atmosphere was at once elegant and lethargic.

But he recognized her accent, somewhere between California, Paris, and Saigon.

"I'll have some too," he volunteered. He had been drinking scotch. The attendant handed him a flute, and he raised it to his seating companion. "Well, here's to the lovely sea!"

"Yes, to the sea." She raised her flute but made no gesture to clink his. She sipped politely, then turned once more to her sea below. The plane quietly hummed.

When he had boarded at Narita, she was already there at 5C, leafing through an old issue of *National Geographic*. Between them a laconic concord, one that might have lasted for the duration, all the way to Ho Chi Minh city, or Saigon once upon a time, if he hadn't tapped her on the arm.

But now—now, with several shots of scotch in him, he wanted to talk. No, he needed to talk. She, with her guarded air, however, presented a challenge.

He emptied his glass and cleared his throat. "Có phải cô là người Việt Kiều?" he asked, a gambit—you must be a Vietnamese expat?

She looked at him and smiled. "Wow, you speak Vietnamese!" in a southern Vietnamese accent, and she said: "Việt kiều," and chuckled as if she hadn't thought about it herself.

"First time back?" he asked.

"First time," she said at length, as if measuring the weight of its meaning. "Yes . . . but how did you know?"

"You seemed nervous," he smiled. "You've been reading the *National Geographic* for at least two hours, and that mag is not known for its literary prowess."

She laughed. "Very perceptive," she said. "And a polyglot."

"Hardly. You speak French and English. You are too."

"But you don't have to. People like me, we learn another language to survive."

"I see. I have a few Việt kiều friends," he offered. "I know about their worries. But things have changed quite a bit, as you may already know." Then, through his American accent, he added, "tất cả là tốt đẹp." All is good and beautiful.

"I doubt that," she said. A neutral and measured voice. "*Có cái đẹp, có cái xấu.*" There's good, there's bad.

A wrong thing to say, he realized almost immediately. In his line of work, it helps to act fast and redirect the flow. "You're right, of course," he said with sympathy. "There's so much that country needs to do in order to move forward." Then he changed the subject. "It's just that it's a vast improvement since I was a foreign exchange student there a dozen years ago in Hanoi."

She stayed mute.

"May I ask if you're on vacation, or is it business?" he tentatively asked.

"My oldest son," she answered. "He's an architect in Saigon working on a big construction project. He invited me. Plus, I donated to an organization that protects and educates poor and at-risk young women. So I plan to see how they're doing."

She leaned forward and, with long, elegant fingers, straightened the back of her silk blouse. Her shoulder-length hair was streaked with gray. Her perfume, the smell of intricate oils, water lilies, and lady apple, reached his nostrils and his childhood memories surged—summer afternoons in the garden, a misty spray from a hose, the cheerful melody from an ice cream truck, and the sounds of his father's laughter.

Here was someone he imagined Thuy-Le would eventually grow into. Gray hair came but the beauty stayed, or rather, it was fading at its own leisure. He could easily see his seating companion as a young woman riding her bicycle along tree-lined boulevards in her white ao dai dress on the way to school. With those sparkling eyes and dimples, many heads must have turned.

"And you?" she asked. "Where are you from? Your Vietnamese, it's very good, by the way. Even got a northern accent."

"Boston. Born and bred, but not the stuck-up, blue blood kind," he said.

"Boston!" she said. "My second son is at Harvard right now, political science major. He's thinking of going into law."

"Wow, Harvard man. I'm impressed. Only made it to Yale myself."

"Oh! What coincidence," she said, eyes widened. "Tommy, the one inviting me, he goes there! I mean went there. You're alumni! I'll introduce you when we land."

"Wow," he said. He shouldn't have lied, a bad habit, but now it had worked, hadn't it? He felt as if she were looking at him with new eyes, this new connection with her son. "I can't believe you're old enough to have children in college, let alone architects and lawyers."

She gave a little laugh. "Believe it, young man. I'm old. Like the old lady and the sea."

"Hardly," he said. "Hemingway would have retitled his masterpiece as the 'Eternal Maiden and the Sea' if he wrote about you." Which made her laugh. "But you must be very proud. I mean, with such smart children," he added.

She studied her flute against sunlight. She hadn't sipped much since the second pouring. She was drinking now. "Sorry," she said. "I didn't mean to boast. What about you? What do you do? How did someone from Boston end up in Hanoi?"

He looked at his Rolex: a good three hours from the destination. "It's too long a story," he feigned. "A story of broken romance, I mean. I don't want to bore you."

"Oh!" she said, sounding suddenly mischievous. "I don't mind, I love a good romance. Absolutely."

She started to arrange herself so that she could better face him, her back against the window, a pillow tugged between her and the armrest, the blanket on her lap. "I promise to not look at the boring *National Geographic* again if you tell your story. You talk. I listen."

"Ok," he said, matching her enthusiasm. "Not sure how good, but it's a sad one. And remember, don't say I didn't warn you." Then he raised his near empty glass above his head and shook it so as to catch the stewardess's attention. "Miss, we need a refill for the road."

Years ago, a young foreign student fell in love with a young Vietnamese woman in Hanoi. The young man had come with little expectations and first saw the city as if in a dream: moss-covered villas and sputtering motorbikes and squatting old men with unfiltered cigarettes dangling from their mouths, the languid city drenched in sunlight and the quiet nights lit by lamp lights and the old ballads sung through open windows from which incense smoke wafted—it was all like a mist on which he drifted, unmoored.

But then there was that winter, which was unexpectedly cold. No snow but the cold, through the humid air, got to the bones, the marrow. A morning in late November and he saw her in the lecture hall. He watched with fascination as the young woman rubbed her hands together—wasn't it at that moment, when she raised her hands to her mouth to breathe warm air through cupped fingers, that she stole his heart?

He knew it the way he knew he would always love raw oysters that first time he swallowed one at seven, that cool, lemony texture slithering down his throat, leaving a salty-sweet aftertaste. Likewise, her hands rubbing in that cold morning sparked the amber into a fire in his heart.

"I hadn't fallen in love with anyone in high school, nor the two years in college, for that matter. Crushes, sure, and a few fell in love with me. But in my junior year in Hanoi, of all places, love wrestled and pinned me to the ground, as the Vietnamese expression goes."

Why Vietnam? Maybe he always wanted to visit the place that haunted his father. Maybe he just needed to get away from stuffy Boston. In any case, when the country opened up after the trade embargo was lifted, he went in, backpacking first, then applying for the exchange program the next year. His father experienced horror in Nam, but him? "I guess I found romance instead."

"She must have been very beautiful," the woman said.

"Oh yeah. Still is, I'm sure," he said. "Thuy-Le was so different. There was, I don't know, an inner peace, a stillness in her, and it made her extraordinarily beautiful. All the boys, and I think some of the teachers, too, had crushes on her. But I courted her. I asked her to teach me Vietnamese in exchange for English lessons. A good bargain, there were very few foreign students at that time. She'd wanted to improve her language skills. She was ambitious. And she laughed at all my stupid jokes."

The woman laughed, too. "Well, humor's important."

But he was in love with the city too, couldn't separate the love affairs from that delicious sense of displacement. How to describe the strangeness of living in a city that was shrouded in shadows after sundown, and in many of its houses, oil lamps and candles lit up crowded rooms; a barely lit city, cigarettes dangling from skinny, old men talking, leaning over balconies. So much beauty in the austere life. In memories, he saw a stained tea thermos and a few cups, a cassette deck, shadows flitting against whitewash walls, a writing desk, a bed with a thin blanket and two pillows; his studio apartment. In memories, too, as in a still life, through an open window, he saw an old man mumbling prayers to the dead as he held a candle in front on his ancestral altar through an open window. On the street, a few bicycles with burning joss sticks stuck in their wheel's pokes served as headlights as they rolled down an empty street, and incense-wafted air turned the entire city into a Buddhist temple. Somewhere in another apartment, a mother sang an old wistful lullaby to calm her crying baby. Elsewhere, an argument. How, indeed, to talk about that feeling of being so out of your elements, and yet it felt like swimming in some mysterious water?

It all still held him captive despite the years. The way they slow-danced to folk music with the flickering oil lamp in his studio when the electricity was out, which was often—the monochord zither echoing nostalgically from an old cassette deck—and their shadows on the wall, and the furtive movement of the mosquito net in the night breeze, the window opened to the dark streets. So vivid were these flashbacks that he sometimes referred to it as post-romantic stress syndrome. But it sounded pretentious, he now told his seating companion, since it was his father who fought in that war and experienced trauma.

Then it all ended. Theirs, after all, was a covert romance: on and off, they managed to live together for almost a year in his small apartment by the Hoàn Kiếm Lake, hiding the fact from the authorities. Her two roommates lied for her. It was illegal back then to visit foreigners' homes overnight, and her parents, who lived in Thai-Binh, didn't know. "She was really afraid of what her parents might do if they'd found out. That was our fight. She kept trying to hide us. I kept complaining of the secretive, restrictive Vietnamese ways. I'm afraid I said some mean things."

That, and how Thuy-Le aggravated him by failing to tell him that she loved him each time he confessed his love. She often would just blush and turn away or say nothing. The last time he had said this, she'd wept. Then she said it: "I love you, too, Mark, very much."

That was the only time she ever said it, but the way she said it, it broke his heart. "What's wrong?" he'd asked, but she hid her face in his chest and sobbed. He came home the next day to find all of her belongings gone. She left no trace. She was back in Thai-Binh somewhere, and her roommates were no help. He didn't know where to find her.

"I should have said I wanted to marry her," he said presently, coming out of a trance. "Maybe that's what she wanted. But after what happened with my parents—their messy divorce—I wasn't too keen on it. I was too young, besides. I mean, I was going to get my MBA after graduating. I didn't give her clear options. And I was leaving, going back to the States in a few months, so I couldn't promise her anything. We didn't discuss it." What he meant to say was he could only see the world through his eyes and failed to see what she saw, but he didn't say it out loud, this flaw: his cowardice; his centrality.

The woman said nothing, but he could tell she was listening the way she looked at him; she was giving him permission. "So, a few months after classes ended, and having failed to find her, my visa ran out. I came home, got my history degree, then got my MBA right after. Now, I'm based in Tokyo selling cosmetic products to wealthy Southeast Asians. I go to Vietnam often, but I've more or less stopped looking for her. I was told she was married and living in Paris. I mean, I have a Japanese girlfriend now."

The woman nodded.

"But then last week," he said. He paused to take a sip of the scotch. ". . . Last week, the phone rang. It was Thuy-Le. She said 'Mark?' and just like that, my heart nearly stopped. It felt like nothing had changed."

They didn't talk long. Indeed, she had been married and living in Paris, but got divorced last year. She said very little about it, but she was now living in Saigon with her child. She met a mutual friend of theirs who gave her his number. She wanted to see him again.

"She said she had something to tell me," he said. His friend took a picture of mother and son. Her son, he said, looked a lot like him at that age.

"You're still very much in love with her," his seating companion said, but it was not a question.

He was going to deny it. But he looked at her. "I never stopped," he barely managed as tears brimmed in his eyes. True, he no longer searched for her, but he couldn't help being reminded of Thuy-Le each time he went to Vietnam on business trips. The nape of a slender neck in an open window, the pealing laughter of a young woman in a candle-lit restaurant, the silhouette of a devout worshipper burning incense in the Buddhist temple's hall—all led to memories of his first love. "I think Thuy-Le still loves me, too. But I don't know what to do. Michiko . . . As open as we are to one another, I never told Michiko about the phone call. The photo. Thuy-Le is waiting for me with her little boy at the airport."

The woman nodded. Silence slowly reasserted itself. He lifted his glass, but his hand shook. He put the flute back down and smiled apologetically while his seating companion studied him. "Well," she said finally, her tone upbeat. "It's a good story. I see now why you speak Vietnamese so well. But I can tell you that it's not a sad story. It's an unfinished story. And you deserve cold champagne, I think." She made a sign to the stewardess, who was walking down the aisle with a tray of drinks. "I'm having some more, too."

"Thuy-Le's little boy's almost ten. His name is Laurent. She wouldn't tell me much, but I couldn't help wondering if . . ." he said before stopping himself. "No," he said quickly, "better not get ahead of myself."

She handed him a tissue from her purse. "Thank you," he said. "You've been very kind to listen. I feel much better. *Cám ơn cô.*"

"*Không có chi,*" she smiled and briefly rested her hand on his wrist, but the sadness remained in her eyes. "It makes me feel better too. I'm glad to know that a happy ending is waiting at our destination."

He wanted to believe her. But he didn't dare envision it. He didn't want to think how the story would end and what it entailed. "Okay," he said and pretended to be relaxed and stretched his arms above his shoulders. "Enough about me. Now, we're getting to your story."

"My story?"

They were flying toward towering cumuli, a huge forest of luminous forms, and light streaked and streamed in from the windows to set faces ablaze. A few passengers pulled down their windows. "I bet you left on the first wave," he said, squinting a little to read her face.

"First wave? Ah, I see. Plane and helicopter people, right? Before the communist tanks rolled into Saigon? No. No such luck. Boat person, I'm afraid. More like second wave. It would have been . . ." She took a sideways glance out the window, her hand shading over her eyes. "Do you mind if I tell you later, when I'm ready?"

"Of course not," he said quickly. He knew of Vietnam's troubles, of course, its past horrors—refugees, boat people, reeducation camps. But the country he went to on regular business trips was one with shiny high-rises and cyber cafes and neon-lit billboards selling Toyota and Coca-Cola and Tiger Beer. It didn't occur to him, considering her comportment, her slight French accent, her excellent English, that she was someone who might have experienced the worst of the Cold War era. It came to him then why she'd been intensely studying that sea.

"You don't have to," he said. "I mean, if you don't feel comfortable, we can talk about . . ."

"No, no," she said, and he could see that she was trembling. But she gathered herself. "It's all right. It's only fair. I will give an abbreviated version."

The stewardess placed two small plates of mixed nuts on their trays, and he was glad he had something to munch on so as to not look at her.

"After the war ended, my husband and I stayed, thinking that young, apolitical academics wouldn't be affected under the new regime," she said after taking a sip of the champagne. "Like you, I taught English. My father also taught it. He practiced it with Graham Greene, in fact, when Greene was living in Saigon and working on that famous novel. My husband taught math. But soon after the war, we lost our jobs. The new government confiscated our house and sent a few of our friends to reeducation camps. We would be next, we figured, so we left by boat about a year after the war ended. Two boats actually, because there wasn't enough space in the first."

She drank a little bit more champagne and gathered herself. "So my husband took our oldest daughter and left. He was always too logical.

He wanted to make sure the statistics were in our favor—that we have a better chance at surviving. I was very mad at him and said some mean things. A week later, I took Tommy and left with my cousin's family. I was pregnant with Phillip, my second son. The whole time, I prayed and I prayed. We made it to the Philippines. They . . . didn't. No news. Nothing. An entire boat, over a hundred people, gone."

It felt as if they were suspended high above the earth, above the clouds, and not moving forward at all. He remained very quiet. He felt a little stupid, having gone on and on about his broken romance. "I'm really sorry," he said finally. "How awful."

"It happened a long time ago," she sighed. "Even so, my mind plays tricks on me. I sometimes fantasize that my husband is raising my daughter in another country—that he is mad at me for things that I said and decided not to find me, find us. Isn't that crazy?"

"No, not at all," he offered. "How else would we go on, I mean, if we don't invent something to hope for?"

She nodded and glanced briefly out the window. "When we were drifting, I missed the simplest things: the sounds of children's laughter, a cold drink, anything on the radio besides static," she said. But she straightened herself. Her voice was lighter, upbeat. "But that's an old story. I survived. My sons survived. I remarried. We went on."

"And now—now, you're coming home, after so many years."

"Now I'm going for a visit after over three decades," she corrected him. "I also donated to an orphanage in the Mekong Delta, and shelters for returning trafficked victims. And I really want to see them, all those at-risk children, see how they're doing."

He'd flown over this ocean many times, but it had never before taken on an ominous aspect. With closed eyes, he could see the woman and her son jostling for space on one of those decrepit, crowded fishing boats bobbing on the water, no land in sight. Then he imagined Thuy-Le, pregnant and alone. He imagined her taking the place of the older woman instead on that boat. He clenched his fist and shut his eyes for fear of crying—it came to him as a shock that his love had such depth. "I didn't go to Yale," he said suddenly. "I don't know why I lied."

"Oh!" said the woman, surprised, and studied his face. But she quickly recovered. "Hey! That's okay," she offered and as if to prove it, she reached out to pat his hand and patted it repeatedly. He held it.

"We're screw-ups. My dad—me," he barely managed to say, before he covered his face in his palm and wept. "I lied a lot to Thuy-Le. Maybe I knew I wasn't ready for marriage, but I talked about the future in such sure ways. Maybe that was why . . ."

The woman studied him. He still hadn't let go of her hand. "Listen," she whispered. "If there's one thing I understand well, it's how rare second chances really are. To fall in love with someone and have that love reciprocated, you're already blessed. To lose it and get another chance, well, you must act on it. It's no good for anyone involved if you don't."

He nodded repeatedly with his eyes shut, lest he embarrass himself by crying again. He continued to grip the woman's hand, however, as she talked, and only let go when he heard the sounds of a cart with its clinking bottles and squeaking wheels going up the aisle.

It was near dusk outside, and behind the clouds, the sun was crimson red. A warm glow spread inside the cabin, and the aromas of baked bread and grilled meat permeated the air. It was almost time for dinner. His stomach growled.

"You okay now?" She handed him another tissue.

"Yes," he smiled meekly at her. "You've been so kind. And you? Are you okay?"

"I'm fine," the woman sniffed, wiping her eyes. He hadn't realized that she'd been crying, too. "But a little drunk. Usually, I don't drink more than one or two glasses before dinner. But I don't even know if it's breakfast or lunch or what, back in San Francisco."

"Well," he deadpanned, "I hate to tell you this, but San Francisco's pretty far behind." She looked at him and laughed. "And," she added, "apparently, so is Tokyo."

The pilot's low, authoritative voice came on the loudspeaker, announcing the remaining time of their flight. "The humidity in Ho Chi Minh city is eighty-five percent, and the temperature 30.5 degrees

Celsius. That's a cool 87 degrees Fahrenheit. I'll update as we near the destination." There was a collective groan in the cabin, followed by sporadic laughter.

"God," said the woman, shaking her head. "I don't know if I can take that heat." He laughed. But she looked at him. "You know," she said, her voice earnest. "I'm not afraid of the past. I made my peace. It's going back to a place that's gone on without me—that's a little scary. So many friends and relatives have scattered. I have more relatives in California and Paris than in Vietnam."

"Well, I have more friends in Saigon and Hanoi and Tokyo than I do in Boston. So welcome to the twenty-first century."

She laughed.

"We haven't been properly introduced," he offered. "My name is Mark. Mark Alexander. I went to Northwestern. An average student, but a smart-mouth. And I can show you around if Tommy's too busy working," he offered. "I know a great pho soup place on the old Pasteur Street."

"I'm Phuong-Anh Harris. But you call me Anne, easier on the tongue. And that's very sweet of you." Her smile was warm, but he wasn't sure if she were entirely convinced of his sincerity.

"Seriously," he said. He needed her to believe him. He wanted to make her happy, too. For he could see now what was at the destination: amid the milling, sweating crowd at the arrival gate, a woman in a green ao dai dress holding the hand of a shy, brown-haired boy in school uniform as she anxiously scanned the faces of arriving passengers. He felt breathless with anticipation. "What can I tell you—what can I do to make you feel more at ease?" he said. "Please—please ask me for anything."

Muni Diaries
Sex on the Bus, Love Down the Avenue

1 *9 Polk*
From my journal, date April 23, 1995.

"Two prostitutes on the 19. See them regularly on the corner of Polk and Post. The best of friends. One white, one Black. Today, the Black one was looking really beat-up, her left leg was in a cast sticking out as she sat on a wheelchair. The other stood next to her. The bus took five minutes to lower the mechanical lift down to let the wheelchair up. What stood out (and why I am writing this down) was this very beautiful white cockatoo perching on the cast, going back and forth and squawking. When the young woman in the wheelchair was being lifted up the bus, her friend had to let the bird perch on her shoulder. On the bus now, and secured, the bird was let back on its owner's cast. I eavesdropped: the two talked about their pimp, who was mean to them. (The bird still pacing on the cast!) And they also talked about how mean this muscular girl Purple Rose on Larkin and Post was, who eventually took their corner. The pimp and Purple Rose had a fight, and Purple Rose beat him up. So now the three lost their corner. But they were happy: 'PR roughed that bitch up. She kicked his ass good,' the woman with the cast kept repeating. They were both laughing hysterically over the fact that their pimp was sent to the ER."

And no. I didn't find out whether PR also sent her to ER. Or, was she hit by a car? Or, more likely, her pimp?

Whatever might have caused the broken leg, the best part of this vignette was this. From my note: "When the two were ready to get off the bus on Polk and Jackson, and as the bus driver unstrapped the wheelchair, the cockatoo went nuts. Its golden crests raised up and down as if in warning as it flapped its wings wildly while screeching: 'Kick his ass! Kick his ass! Kick his ass!'"

The bus driver, I remember, and all the passengers, we all laughed.

"Yeah, honey, he got his sorry ass kicked so hard, he flew all the way back to Mississippi," replied one of the two women, barely able to control her laughter. "Lord, oh lord, he flew, all right."

The cockatoo still haunts my imagination, its golden crests forming question marks over its handsome head. In dreams, in reveries, it paces back and forth on that woman's cast, squawking, flapping its beautiful wings, its crests raising and falling at various intervals, while telling everyone to keep kicking the pimp's ass.

I think a story might be told from the point of view of the bird as it witnessed the famous fight. A retired lawyer, I tried my hand at creative writing, but couldn't finish this story at a writing workshop and gave up. So I am relinquishing it to you, dear reader.

What are its favorite phrases besides "Kick his ass!"? What else did it see from its perch over the young woman's bed all those lurid nights? What does it long for? What are its motivations, its quirks?

In any case, I think it would be a nice gesture to me, if you're writing a story about it, to name it Norbert.

14 Mission

I am twelve, and Rob de Leon, brown hair, blue eyes, is thirteen. We have been friends for three years, ever since that first week when I walked into our fifth grade classroom fresh from the refugee camp of Guam and sat behind him, and he tried to pronounce my Vietnamese name and failed miserably, which made me giggle for the first time in a long time.

Rob taught me how to swear. We lived on the same street, it turned out, two blocks from each other. We tossed a football on our quiet street after school, annoying the neighbors, making the dogs bark with our raucous laughter.

Today, we are going to the Tower Theater on Mission Street. A Saturday matinee that even refugee kids like me can afford: for a dollar you get to see two movies, back-to-back. And it's *Planet of the Apes* and *Beneath the Planet of the Apes*.

For the matinee, Rob wears faded overalls and a white tank top, his trademark weekend clothing. He is muscular and handsome. And girl crazy. He wears no underwear and tells everyone about it. "Let it breathe," he says and winks, pushing his front forward to create enough space so that I can see that he's serious.

I can also smell him, that whiff of boy musk. It overwhelms my nostrils, especially as Charlton Heston and Linda Harrison are doing their thing on the beach. Then I notice quick movements in the dark: Rob is jerking himself furiously. I hear him panting, see him tensing up. The apes shoot after a fleeing Heston on horseback, and Rob shoots his wad. His whole body trembles, his stomach tightens as if he's got shot—then that unmistakable spasm during orgasm to be followed by tremors of pure pleasure. After a few seconds, he sighs, then looks over at me as I stare at him, astonished. He giggles.

After the matinees, we get on the 14 Mission to head home. We sit near the back of the bus where it is empty. His right hand goes back inside his overall, and he is playing with himself while looking lazily out the window, surely his head is full of violent apes chasing a sexy girl in a leather loincloth as he continues to beat his own monkey.

When he sees me scowling at him, he smiles: "Next time I'll let you borrow my overalls. I have extra. You can't do shit with tight jeans."

That smile in the sunlight: well, it dazzles.

For about twenty minutes, we don't talk. Except for when I have to warn him that someone is coming down the aisle. But he keeps playing with himself.

I think about wearing his overalls. Though to be more honest, sniffing it.

Next to me, Rob shoots his wad inside his overalls again. He moans. "Fuck!" he whispers. His hair falls over his eyes as he turns to me and whispers: "Fuck. It's better the second time."

"Hey, horny ape. Go home and do laundry!"

He ignores my comment. "Hey, Refugee Boy," he says. "Let's go again next Saturday to see *Escape from the Planet of the Apes*."

Then without warning, Rob wipes some of his cum on my jeans, right above the knee, and laughs.

"Fuck!" I yell. "Ew!" I punch him on his arm. Hard.

"Don't wash it, okay. I want to see this cum spot next time as a mark of our friendship."

"You're fucking gross, man!"

Rob continues laughing. Apparently, he finds smearing me with his boy juice hilarious.

I start to giggle, too.

His cum, shaped like an exclamation point, is drying on my jeans. Underneath that spot, my skin tingles as heat rises to my face. Robert de Leon falls asleep next to me, his handsome head resting against the window, hair gleaming and glittering in the sunlight, and before I know it, I, too, follow him into that midsummer afternoon dream.

Rob's cum spot stayed on my jeans for weeks. One day at school, he saw me wearing them and smirked like a dog recognizing its fire hydrant.

We never saw *Escape from the Planet of the Apes*. After junior high, we went to different high schools. Soon, we fell out of touch. But once in a while, years after that moment, whenever I drove by the old neighborhood, I would think of him, of the football being tossed back and forth between us, of all those lazy afternoons exploring the hillsides with our small group of friends.

And after all these years, that smell of buttered popcorn in that old theater mixed with Robert de Leon's musky odors will aways remind me of my early summers in America.

49 Van Ness

The 49 meanders—mostly up and down Van Ness Ave. Rarely do I sit in the back of any bus, and definitely not on the 49, considering the rough crowds that tend to get on and off from Market to Gary. Except that one easy-pleasy afternoon. Why? Who the hell knows. A gentle breeze maybe, and the blue, blue sky? A gentleness in the air, maybe? And the bus was mostly empty.

I had left work early, and the windows in the back were wide open wide. The wind blew. They beckoned.

In my mid-twenties, with a nonexistent love life, I was interning at a law firm for a year now and moving slowly up that ladder. I sat at the furthest end, on a long bench, a six-seater, and it spanned the bus's entire girth. I was wearing my gray suit, but I had taken off my tie and unbuttoned the shirt to the chest. Occasionally, I gazed down at the folder of a case I had been researching for my boss, but mostly I was looking out the window, thinking of nothing. I barely noticed a couple in their mid-thirties who made their way back and sat on the opposite end of the bench. He was good-looking, if sleazy—blue eyes and dirty brown hair with a goatee. She was on the thin side with a slightly dazed look and shiny blond hair that was surely a bad dye job. I ignored them until a strange movement from the corner of my eyes made me look.

He, eyes closed, was listening to music on his Walkman while his woman got down on her knees and began blowing him. What reached my ears, amidst the constant roar of the bus engine, was his moaning and Latin jazz. And if you didn't see that woman's head bobbing up and down his rather sizable pole, you'd think the Girl from Ipanema was giving him infinite joy.

I cleared my throat in meek protest. He opened his eyes and looked sideways at me with dreamy eyes, a smirk on his face. Then, as if not sure what I wanted, or maybe not caring, out his window he recast his gaze.

The woman, meanwhile, got more outrageous. She got up, lifted her skirt, and pulled down her blue lace panties that must have seen the earlier part of the Reagan administration, and started riding her companion.

Before I knew it, I heard myself stammering like a schoolmarm, "Uhm, excuse me!" Immediately, I wondered: why did I do that? Why call attention to myself? Why didn't I just get up and move to another seat?

Too late.

This time I got the woman's attention. She stopped her knob-hopping, so to speak, and looked over at me. Eyes dazed, lipstick slightly smeared, and in a voice full of lust yet foreboding, "Hold your horses, hon. Be with you in a minute."

1 California

As usual, it's crowded on the 1 California. It's Saturday morning, the bus is heaving itself up to Nob Hill on its way from Chinatown. Hooked by a metal pole that often falls off from being vicariously connected to its overhead electric wires, the bus trudges up and down steep hills almost all the way toward the sea.

Greg, a colleague at my law firm, used to call it the "Slow Bus to China." One could indeed get seasick the way it bobbed and waddled. Standing-only space that morning: which meant a lot of noisy, old Asian ladies jostling for room, their plastic bags of groceries grazing against your legs.

I was twenty-eight then. Still convinced that I was bi-curious, by which I mean I realized I could still find women attractive, but increasingly I gravitated toward men. But how would I know, since up until then, I was only drawn to one man and hadn't touched another since college?

It could have been a fluke, I kept thinking, the one that I once loved. Aren't we all fluctuating on some spectrum like Kinsey postulated? I dated a few women, and the one long-term relationship, by which I mean two years, I had with an older woman ended in mutual disdain and dissatisfaction.

Still too shy to act on my own, I became keenly aware of how much I increasingly appreciated male beauty. Albeit from a distance.

On Jackson and Larkin, a man got on. Dirty blond, late twenties with green eyes, torn jeans, blue faded T-shirt clinging to a well-defined chest. Brief eye contact, and my blood quickened. I looked away, but not before I caught a smirk on his face.

He was standing near the front of the bus. I was standing in the middle. Half the population of Kowloon seemed to be standing between us.

More people climbed up. Hot Guy pushed himself toward my direction. I turned sideways and grabbed the upper headrail with both hands and pressed myself toward the single-seated Chinese lady so as to let him go past. The old lady scowled, not appreciating my crotch so close to her wizened chin, but it couldn't be helped.

Except Hot Guy didn't squeeze past me to get to the back of the bus, where there was more standing room. No, he stood behind me, raised one arm to grab the overhead rail, his torso on my back, then as more people got on, he raised his other arm and grabbed the metal bar and pressed his body against me. Our hands touching; he was, in effect, spooning me in front of a mostly elderly Chinese audience.

More passengers came up. They pushed past us. Hot Guy found an excuse to rub and drub as we climbed Nob Hill. Worse, he was breathing down the back of my neck.

I was horrified. I was thrilled.

But mostly, I wanted to bring one hand down to cover the growing bulge in my pants before it poked the old lady in her right cheek. But I was immobilized. Every time the bus came to a jolting stop, I could feel the heat of his bulge against the crack of my ass.

Sweat began to pour down my temples. My heart beat like a tom-tom in my throat. I gulped. Yet I said nothing. Then I felt his tongue on my neck. It sent electric jolts down my spine. "Yum," he whispered. "Salty . . . sweet."

My knees buckled. The hair on my arms rose in response. My grip on the metal bar above me was that of a man hanging on over some unfathomable abyss. His breath on my ear, the nape of my neck. He licked again; I bit down for fear of crying out loud.

But then the bus lurched to a stop at Clay and Powell.

"Too bad," he whispered. "Work awaits. If today were Saturday, nothing would have saved you."

Then he was gone.

Nob hadn't topped Hill and it was, alas, all over.

The man left an impossible void. Yet it was not that hot, hot man that I missed in the aftermath. No, not exactly. In the absence of his sheltering body, my mind took accounting of all my losses: the insularities of family life when I was a Vietnamese child, and friendship from the high school friend with whom I fell in love and who didn't reciprocate in a way that would have given me closure, and that sadness that turned into silence between my parents and I, and the way in which my own life was both promising and yet unsatisfying at the same time, how the future was both exciting and frightening as I navigated my world alone.

Then there came this irrefutable self-knowledge: I definitely prefer men. I stood there feeling both sorrow and inspiration. So this is what it is to accept one's fate?

To be honest, after so many sultry nights, so many sheltering bodies, so many heartbreaks, I still feel that void to this day, wishing that long-ago Thursday was somehow the beginning of a long, sweetly remembered weekend.

5 Fulton

The Old World from which I fled was like a bento box. Proper behaviors are expected and enforced, its mindset unwavering despite a difficult mass exodus that relocated so many of us to the West. Little Saigon communities across the US over time became more restrictive and more conservative than the real Saigon, by far. It's as if fearing losing its roots, the exile community became entrenched, preserving culture instead of creating it, all the while casting a nostalgic gaze toward what's lost and gone.

In that enclave, Confucian values are exaggerated to show unity. Saving face and showing off are two strong organizing principles that trump freedom of expression, and nowhere would this be more conspicuous than at a Vietnamese-American wedding, where gossip abounds.

"So-and-so's son didn't finish college and this big tech company showed up on campus to beg him to work for them. He's that smart. He's that good"—is contrasted with controlled whispers, "So-and-so's daughter got pregnant at seventeen." And "Oh my god, Mrs. T's son came out as gay. Gay! Shocking!"

And—"That man over there, he came with nothing, and now he owns three mansions and a big high tech company. His son is at MIT. Incredible."

"Shhh! Oh my god, sister, did you know, Mr. S is now living downstairs and his best friend is shagging his wife upstairs? So shameful."

I am bringing this up because, for the longest time, I was my parents pride and joy. The corporate lawyer who handles high profile cases and drives an expensive Porsche.

But secretly, I fantasized about being a go-go dancer. No, not in real life, because, well, a well-paid corporate lawyer cum go-go dancer might run-run into his colleagues if he moonlights in some sleazy dive in San Francisco in a worn leather thong. It would be quite unbecoming, so to speak.

Despite its global fame, San Francisco, without land for suburbs except to the south, has always been a small city. Imagine stripping onstage and your boss shows up to rub a Hamilton on your taut abdomen, or worse, your secretary with a few Jacksons wanting some extra special Magic Mike action. Or maybe this vision from hell: somebody from Little Saigon, or worse, a closet queen of my parents' circle, looking up at his "nephew's" ass.

Yes, I imagined it and got thrills from it, I practiced dancing in front of the mirror—but for a long time, in front of the looking glass it stayed.

But then one night . . .

. . . I've been jogging early every morning. Plus, for over two years now, I have taken up weightlifting four or five times a week. I became addicted to working out. I even got a trainer at the gym, and with his regimen, my body became sculpted, with well-defined stomach muscles and a well-rounded chest. I posed nightly in the mirror, and I saw no corporate lawyer. I saw a stripper staring back at me.

That night, bored out of my mind from overwork on a business merger draft, I started a Craigslist post just to amuse myself: "Private dancer for hire. 5'9", 150 lbs, Asian. Muscular, very cute & friendly. Dimples and round, firm ass. Uncut. Oil me up. Pat me down. Play with my six-pack. Make me serve drinks for your guests in my leather thong. Or without. Safe only." Included are two photos of my round ass and my well-defined torso.

Was I aware that I had posted on M-for-M on Craigslist? Yes and no. Certainly I wasn't expecting the avalanche for missives that followed. Many willing to pay. I promptly ignored them all, until after work the next evening after working out at the gym.

One email in particular caught my attention: "Wealthy. Very private. Come dance for me. No other guests. Will respect your limits. Your services will be handsomely rewarded. Interested?"

Succinct. Precise. I like that. Not that I needed the money, but when you fantasize about whoring yourself out, part of the turn-on is getting paid.

We negotiated the terms. 300 bucks. No sex. Touching okay. Kissing okay.

I took the 5 Fulton. I rang the bell on a very modern house on the hill.

Did I expect a very handsome man in his forties? No. But there he was—a tall man in a gray turtleneck with well-coiffed black hair and the bluest eyes. He was stunning.

Would you like me . . .
No. It's my show.
Yes sir.
Strip. And get on the ottoman.

I never wanted anyone so badly in all my adult life. He watched from the comfort of his sofa, drinking a martini.

He kept his distance. He drank; I gyrated. I danced away all the old world. I thrust and bent, I chased away all the old shame.

He got up. He made another martini. Long elegant fingers like those of a pianist. Then he approached me.

Boy, make it extra dirty.
What? What do you mean?
You know what I mean.
Yes, sir.

It took me a while.

Here's your martini, sir.

The martini was regarded through squinted eyes, as if a jeweler an uncut diamond. He took his first sip, his gaze was still on me, my sweaty torso. Then, his smile blossomed into laughter.

In that laugh, I saw a naughty young man, an impish child, a kind person. But also loneliness, someone who attended an Ivy League school, who knew many powerful people, and whose heart had closed its shop a while back.

Sir. May I kiss you?
No. But I will kiss you here.
Yes, sir.
And here.
Yes. Thank you.
Thank you what?
Thank you, sir.

What I want to say in the aftermath was that I wish I hadn't been so needy. He turned cold when I asked for his full name. He was even less impressed when I told him I was an up-and-coming corporate lawyer. That I'd love to see him again.

The play ended.

It was great fun. I'll send you home.
Oh ... it's ok. I can take the bus.
You will not. I've already called my driver. He's waiting downstairs.
Oh! Okay, sure.
There's an envelope on the table by the landing. That was no false advertising. Thank you.

On the ride back, I looked into the envelope. Ten crisp 100 dollar bills. I laughed.

What a windfall, first time out.

The chauffeur, in man his late fifties, studied me in the rearview mirror.

"Sir, is everything all right?"

"Oh, it's all good. Thanks."

"In case you're wondering, he's not famous. Just very rich. And very private. If you don't mind, just a fair warning: most likely, you'll never hear from him again. But for what's it's worth, he sounded very pleased."

When I looked out of the limo's window, I saw the 5 Fulton meandering up the avenue, its bus driver yawning a yawn of pure resignation.

I started to pray for the first time in a long time.

Dear Mr. Craigslist,
Please find me a real boyfriend. Someone like that Mystery Man. Please! And I'll light incense to the Buddhas and ancestors and ask them to bless you, and for him (and his guests) I'll dance, free, every night. I swear. Every fucking night.

Amen.

The J Church—Inbound and Out
I am older now, forty-two, and was in a relationship with a man my

age for over four years, but earlier this evening, we broke up. We have our differences, but the main obstacle for me was his overwhelming sadness, which at times sent him spiraling. A kind, considerate businessman, elegant and compassionate. But also, an insecure man whose world could fall apart due to some careless sentence spoken by an acquaintance at some party.

My upbeat personality itself was taken as an offense when he was down. It was as if being around someone cheerful hurt him. I've seen him wince at the sound of my laughter when I watched a sitcom or when I giggled while talking to a friend on the phone. I could almost hear him thinking: how can you be so damn cheerful when I am this sad?

For those few years I would take the J to see him twice a week, getting out to Noe Valley. And he would try to find parking once a week, mostly on the weekends, at my place on Nob Hill. And when our various travels permitted, we would spend a few days in a mutually designated city due to our international work. But without saying it, we were navigating the much more difficult terrain between two middle-aged, established professional adults working toward a possible life together.

Last summer, we went to Marrakesh. He had to go home first because of work. We had a terrible fight the night he left. And I decided to stay—and I joined a caravan into the Sahara and had a wonderful time.

It is winter now. And late in the evening. I have to rush to get to the J, its arrival sporadic this time of the night, and it's cold out. The bag of books, which I just retrieved from his apartment, is heavy on my shoulder.

I step on dead leaves on the street. I pull up the collar of my coat for extra comfort.

I left quite a few books at his place, and he had meticulously placed them in a faded red Adidas duffle bag for me to take home. Marquez, Didion, Nabokov, and Baldwin vie with Ishiguro, McEwan, and Ondaatje and a host of others to weigh me down. As I walk, predominant on my mind is that Courvoisier I am going to pour for myself when I get home. And I see myself lighting a couple of logs in the fireplace in my rundown Victorian apartment with its quaint but creaky windows that let in too much cold air. I think about playing a few French songs from the '60s and wrapping myself in my chunky gray wool blanket.

A Black teenager sitting on the other side of the aisle. He has been watching me. I don't notice him until he gets up as the train nears the Market and Gough station.

"Yo, man. Here you go." He takes out a couple of Starbucks paper napkins from his jacket and hands them to me. It seems that I have been crying.

I see kindness in his eyes. I take the napkins. "Thank you!" I say and force a smile. Then, by impulse, I reach into my bag of books.

"And this is for you . . . "

The teenager looks at it. "*One Hundred Years of Solitude*," he says. "Man, that's a long, long time to be lonely." The doors slide open. He waves the book in the air then steps out.

• • • •

Bus, Bart, Metro, Pounding the Sidewalk—The Quantum of Desire

None of those bus and metro rides will ever compare to that summer day when I was college-bound, however. My junior year at Mission High, my father received a big promotion at his company and his new position required a long commute to San Jose. After a few months, he'd had enough. He sold our first house in America, a humble three bedroom in a working-class neighborhood, and bought a five bedroom home at the edge of what was then the northern edge of Silicon Valley, complete with a pool winking in the backyard.

I was sixteen going on seventeen. I didn't want to move. Despite the swimming pool and the pastoral view of rolling hills and the wisteria bushes perfuming the garden those languid nights, it was far, far from my beloved city. Making new friends for senior year was not an option, especially when prepping for college. But mostly, I couldn't imagine being torn away from my best friend, who was going to apply to the same university. I argued that to continue going to the city's high school was the right thing to do, even, well, if it meant lying about a change of address and getting up early—at 5:30 each morning, with my mother who worked in the city—to get a ride to BART in Fremont with her, and then transfer at 16th Mission BART before walking to Mission High.

My chances of getting into Berkeley would be greatly diminished had I transferred to another school in the middle of my junior year, I reasoned. My parents relented.

So, trudge we did, my mother and I.

After all these years, long after my parents are gone, I can still see my mother's pained face as she urged me to get up before dawn, her voice low and soft, "Con oi, thuc di con." Or my father's sympathetic gaze as I asked to have a sip of his extra bitter coffee at the breakfast table to shake myself awake (I couldn't back then finish two sips, and resented that bitter taste, but this morning I realized in old age, I prefer coffee more bitter than my father's).

Oh, how I bitched and moaned. A sloth surely would've rolled out of bed faster than me that senior year. But then, all too quickly, it was over. I got accepted into Cal and graduated. School ended. Summer came. No more early morning commute. My parents threw a party. The relatives came. My best friend from school came and stayed for three days. We swam and played guitar and sang and talked of our future together at Cal.

I wanted to study law, just like my paternal grandfather, who went to the Sorbonne.

But before college, I faced a long summer in the suburbs working a part-time at a gas station for pocket money. I was otherwise bored out of my mind.

And I missed my best friend . . . so damn much.

We talked on the phone nightly. We giggled, made silly jokes. We gossiped and bantered for hours. But it had been at least two weeks since we last saw each other. He had planned to come down, but it didn't work out. I offered to come up instead. The plan was to meet him at his house in the morning and we would spend the day exploring. And maybe stay over for the night, as I often did during my senior year.

"We'll bike to Land's End and maybe picnic on the beach. And maybe after, bike up to Chinatown for wonton noodles."

"Sure," he said. "It's a plan."

That night I said to my mother, "Mom, wake me up tomorrow, okay. I'll come with you to the city."

"Are you sure?" she said in a wary voice. "It's a long commute." Then she studied me: "It's not like you won't see each other in the fall."

"It's been a long, long, boring summer. So yes, I'm sure. Mom, please."

Then I woke to find the room heated and bright. I cursed. Either my mother forgot or felt it was too early to wake me. She'd seen me suffer nightly for months preparing for my grueling AP finals in spring, and maybe she thought I needed the extra sleep. Or maybe she thought it was pointless given that I would see my best friend in less than a month at Cal.

For a good minute, I cursed the fate of a suburban teenager without a car. I had let my best friend down; it was unforgivable. Then there came that Scarlett O'Hara moment when she was hungry and in the dirt, holding a turnip in her antebellum hand with a powerful resolve.

As god is my witness, even if I have to walk, I am going to get to the city.

Where we lived, it was a good fifteen miles from the last BART Station, which was then in Fremont. There were two buses that I needed to take.

Between my house to that first bus stop? A mile . . . and an impossible distance.

Why? The bus came by at regular thirty-minute intervals.

I had about twelve minutes to spare. I needed to run to the first stop; fast.

I put on my track suit and tennis shoes, stuffed my wallet and keys in my backpack, and opened the front door to see a blinding sun . . .

Like a fool, running toward some unknown. Stopping twice to catch his breath, palms against knees and gasping for air. A hot morning. The smell of dry grass. Above everything else, the bluest sky. By the time the boy reached the transfer point with less than a minute to spare, his drenched shirt clung to him.

The two passengers on that bus looked askance at a teenager soaking with sweat but smiling back at them as he sat down. An immense sense of relief washed over him. It had felt as if his entire future was dependent on getting to the city before midday, and now he was on his way.

His best friend must be confused, or maybe angry at him for failing to come on time? He balled his fist, thinking of his friend standing there with his two bicycles by the garage waiting for him.

Time passed and did not pass. The bus came, and it was a lonely ride toward Fremont. Now that he was on his way, he was more patient.

On the platform for the San Francisco-bound train, he paced and watched the electric sign above.

"San Francisco Train arriving in 7 minutes"

"San Francisco Train arriving in 5 minutes"

"San Francisco Train arriving in 3 minutes"

Finally, out in the distance, a gray metal snake wound its way on the metal track toward him, and he broke into a smile.

It was cool inside. He sat by the window, and tract houses and dry hills rolled by in a blur. To kill time, the boy reached for his novel in his backpack and pretended to reread *The Old Man and the Sea*—his last AP English assignment—an easy read, but the words didn't make much sense, and all he could remember were sharks taking bites of the man's marlin until there was little left, the sea a trail of blood, and the old man near dead. But yes, he did write about man's determination:

the willpower and sacrifice needed to get what you desire, despite everything. And got an A.

He had taken this train regularly since he moved to the South Bay. But it felt to him as if he was on a new destination, a familiar trek, yet he felt as if going toward some unknown country.

At Civic Center, he took the N out toward Sunset Boulevard where his friend lived. It took another good thirty minutes, and he ran the remaining five blocks until he was standing in front of that whitewashed house with brown window trimmings.

His best friend's mother opened the door and immediately scowled at his appearance. "He's still asleep," she said and opened the door wider for him to come in. "So lazy in the summer." She was, in any case, on her way out, so feel free to wake him up.

Relief washed over him. All was well. He shook his head and smiled. His best friend slept through it all. Probably forgot to set his alarm clock. Definitely not a morning person.

He went to the kitchen, helped himself to a full glass of water, then he went to the bathroom to clean up. He almost laughed out loud: in the mirror, a disheveled boy stared back at him—the cowlick hair, some crust deposits in the corner of one eye, the blue jersey soaked with sweat clinging to a thin, if muscular, frame. There was a reason why his friend's mother scowled: he looked like a tramp.

He wet his hair, washed his face, and brushed his teeth with the toothbrush his friend gave him from his last stay over. He made himself as presentable as possible before he gingerly climbed up the stairs. It was dark inside, and warm. He heard a familiar snore. An odor of musk and sweat and dirty socks permeated the air.

His friend had thrown off the blanket as the day became hotter, and his naked torso was exposed to a small beam of sunlight—the robust chest, the smooth skin glistening in that light.

He stepped closer. He was barely aware of himself when he sat down on the corner furthest away, at the edge, for fear of waking the sleeping boy.

How long did he sit there? A minute? An hour? An eternity?

The bed was a vast, unknown ocean, and he was standing at its shore.

His friend stirred, arms outstretched, deltoids and triceps rippled like rolling knolls under a dancing light. He heard a little moan. His heart beat wildly. He felt as if his very being had melted into the sea. There'll be years of running away from this beatific moment. Years of denying the existence of this place, this ocean, which owned him still. Years of searching for its substitutes, of hiding in others' flesh, and years of failing.

But for now, there is only grace and beauty. And the city outside the windows—its hills dotted with Victorian homes, its streets full of rumbling buses and clanking cable cars—is but a promise yet fulfilled. They are seventeen. The beautiful boy hasn't yet awakened. The first kiss is still to be had; and the heart is still an uncharted terrain, its treble and bass barely heard. The afternoon hasn't yet begun.

The Tree of Life

I usually can speak without notes, but on this occasion, the saddest in my life, I don't think I can speak a word without having written it down.

But first, my family and I want to thank everyone who gathered here today to honor our mother. I am sure she'd fed many of you at one time or another, and hugged a few, and told many a good story, and to a small privileged few, she might have scolded you a few times, telling you to behave and to be good . . .

Many years ago, one of my mentors, a professor from Berkeley, and I were discussing the Vietnam War and its horrors, and he said something along these lines: "Men stand at the ready for battle, at the door of death, but women . . . they stand at the tree of life."

I knew he was talking metaphorically, that these are archetypes of the sexes that form our world, but I, of course, immediately thought of my father and mother.

My father fought in a Vietnam war for twenty-five years, fought until its bitter end. He saw enough death and destruction to last several lifetimes.

And my mother? She grew up in North Vietnam and experienced war and famine, and then she was part of a mass exodus south in 1954, which divided Vietnam in half and led to a long, bitter civil war.

My mother remembered peasants who came into her city during the famine of 1945, begging for food. She was twelve going on thirteen. Since my grandparents were well off and had in their storage a lot of rice, my mother and her older brother decided to make porridge. They made thin gruel, and in the mornings, they scooped as much as they could from their big family pot and fed those who begged near their house. They kept doing it for weeks.

My mother saw dead bodies being scooped up each day on the streets and being carted away. She saw a child sitting up on a pile of dead bodies only to lie back down to die. She saw the police whip a crazed woman who ate parts of a child under a bridge.

But in her retelling: it was the porridge-making that she remembered the most, and the satisfaction she got from being able to feed the hungry.

To feed, to nurture, to protect. To react to harsh reality with kindness and generosity—this is the very essence of my mother.

It made sense, then, that when she moved south and married my father, an army officer for South Vietnam who became a general when I was born, that she would wield her powers as a general's wife to do something for the poor and the needy.

It was in Sadec, deep in the Mekong Delta, where she built an orphanage. She fundraised and cajoled and coaxed the powerful and the rich in the region to donate resources and money, and land, and soon, there it was: two buildings to house orphans and a kitchen in the middle.

I remember how those kids kept calling her *mẹ*, Vietnamese for Mother. And at four, I remember weeping. "But she's not your mother," I would yell. "She's *my* mother."

Of course, she was, in many ways, the closest thing to being a mother to those kids. She housed and fed them. She ate and sang with them. She sent them to school. Over time, she even managed to send some to higher education, and two even made it to Switzerland near the end of the war, on scholarship.

And yes, one later became a doctor in America—the only person, my mother pointed out to me sarcastically, who called her mother "that actually became a doctor."

When the battles got worse, and hospitals were full during the Tet

Offensive, my mother converted half of the orphanage into a makeshift hospital. There, she and the nurses and social workers tended to wounded soldiers, and one of them met a wounded captain, and they fell in love. My mother supported them with a makeshift wedding.

The tree of life.

To love, to protect—my mother never wavered. I used to think of my father in a heroic light as a child. He who flew in helicopters and who called bombs to fall from the sky, and he who jumped down to earth in a parachute—he was like a thunder god, like James Bond, but my mother? Well, she was a true lioness. And when it comes to her family, she was fearless.

Near the end of the war, my father and his army were forced to retreat south from the city of Hue near the DMZ where he was in command. They took amphibious boats south to Danang, and the evacuation was difficult. Many died.

Not knowing if he was alive or not, my mother flew out to Danang from Saigon, and she didn't go empty handed: no, she brought dozens of chickens from the farm we owned on the outskirts of Saigon with her. And she brought rice.

Behind her, rockets rained down from the Hai Van pass onto Danang, killing people, but mother had cooking to do. Under the coconut trees by the beach of the naval base, she set up a makeshift kitchen and waited for her husband and his army to come in. The lady general commanded a few sailors to start building fires, and together they made chicken porridge in big steel drums, and when those landing craft carrying troops arrived, with the men all ravished from hunger and weakened by several days at sea—my mother fed them all.

"Your father was shocked. He didn't expect me to be there," she would later recall, laughing. "But he was so weak that his soldiers had to drag him to shore." Then she'd laugh some more, thinking of the soldiers that she managed to feed. "You should have seen the faces of those young men. The way they ate the porridge. They say, Madam, you saved our lives."

Often, I wondered about my mother. How is it that my mother managed to remain so cheerful and highly functional in the face of all the death and destruction that defined so much of her life in Vietnam, and why didn't those memories of war haunt her in America?

Then it occurred to me that that impulse to protect, that instinct to nurture and save, to put the self in service of others—it formed the very core and spirit of who she was, and it turned out to be her own best medicine against grief. War and death and sadness didn't own her. She, in many ways, owned them: she was always an active agent in the face of calamity.

That is to say, she was busy making soup.

Then the war ended, and it ended badly. And the south lost, and like everyone else who fled as refugees to America, my family lost everything.

We had to start from scratch.

My mother and her sister started working in a hole-in-the-wall on top of the hill in Daly City. My teenage sister helped. My eldest brother worked in a supermarket across the street, and he helped support us too with his meager income while going to high school. I was too young to do anything but sulk and feel bereft and abandoned. I had nightmares. I missed my father who had stayed behind.

Then, a few months after we came to America, news came that my father had made it out of Vietnam, having escaped after us by boat. We rejoiced. We celebrated. He'd survived. But when he arrived, he was a changed man—thin and dark and brooding. And he was a broken man, a defeated man.

Traumatized and haunted by the losses and having seen so much bloodshed, he sat in his bedroom and brooded. Sometimes, in the evening, he would come out to watch the news in the living room. He listened to Walter Cronkite tell him more bad news and drank whiskey and soda on ice. Then he'd retreat to his bedroom in silence.

Surely, those twenty-five years of fighting haunted him—what was it all for?

Sometimes he would join us for dinner. Other times, he ate alone.

He was more or less immobilized by the horror and loss, the humiliation of defeat. That door of death and despair didn't shut after the war ended. It was beckoning him.

My mother fretted. But after half a year or so, she'd had enough. Losing a country and struggling to survive in poverty in another country with three children was stressful enough, but on top of it, here was a husband incapacitated by ghosts.

One night, a furious fight broke out between my parents.

In that little apartment of ours above the restaurant where she toiled, there was a lot of yelling. Shape up, she was screaming at him. Wake up from this damn stupor! She threatened to take the children and leave him all alone if he didn't.

This, mind you, was a woman who earlier, in another country, risked her own life in a war zone and waited on a beach to feed her husband when he swam to shore. A few more fights, and soon after that, things patched up between them, and then late one night, as I slept in the dining room wrapped in a beat-up sleeping bag on a little cot, I heard my parents talking above me.

"Swear to me," she whispered. "You swear to me you will fight to get us out of poverty. *Anh thề đi* . . . You swear to me you will do everything in your power to keep our family fed. Restore us, make us whole again so that this little boy can grow up happy."

My father took his time. Then he said: "I swear to you. I will make sure our children will be provided for."

I remember that moment well. I lay there pretending to be asleep, but I quietly wept. I never shared it with anyone until now, not even with my siblings. But in that moment, I knew: my mother was casting her magic spell. On one level, she was trying to save her family or her marriage, but on a deeper level, she was in fact risking the unity of her family—that which she treasured above all else—in order to save my father once more.

She was steering his gaze away from all the specters of war, steering it toward a brighter future in America—the promise of a good life, of restoration forged from the sheer willpower which she knew existed in him. In essence, she was saying: "Look away from the ghosts and stand with me. Stand with me under this tree of life. Let us tend to it. Let it bear fruits. Let's make us whole again!"

And he did all that he swore to my mother.

Not long after that night, he got a job at the Bank of America. He studied and got a BA in political science, he studied at night school, and through Herculean efforts, got an MBA, and over time, became an assistant VP in the trust department at the bank. After fighting a war in another country for twenty-five years, he was climbing the corporate ladder in another, a feat unheard of among his contemporaries.

His first check bought me three albums that held stamps. I had escaped Vietnam with my treasured stamp collection in a plastic bag, but the heavy albums that housed them had to stay behind. The gifts shocked and delighted me on many levels.

But I was incredibly happy: a home for my beautiful stamps at last— and deep down I knew—my father was indeed fulfilling his promises to my mother . . .

Preparing for today's occasion, my family and I looked at a myriad of photos that spanned the years. And as I looked through them, the story they tell is not sadness, but that of celebration, of a happy life.

The images in America span a good part of over four decades: they tell of housewarming parties, of weddings and graduations, and many a birthday party, not to mention the various European and Mexican vacations and cruises. All together, the images bear witness to our ascendency from that humble beginning as refugees from Vietnam. A sort of American dream, Vietnamese style.

And as I sorted through all of those images that spanned the many happy years—I swear to you, I could almost hear my mother's laughter ringing clear and loud. For she knew she'd triumphed.

- She loved to sing. She sang while working in the kitchen, or else she sang in her little garden.
- She would never admit that she was wrong. She could be sarcastic when corrected. "Of course, you went to Berkeley, that's why you know everything."
- She was a great cook. And instead of saying I love you, or I am sorry, she would say, I fried a fish for you. Eat. And you knew better than to say no. So, even when not hungry, you eat.
- She was a devout Buddhist. Until her health failed her, she lit incense and prayed to Buddha and ancestors nightly. And what did she pray for? Always the same thing: protection and prosperity for her family and clan.
- She knew how to use a gun. And yes, she used it. She once shot at my father for cheating on her with a third-rate singer with big boobs. Somewhere in Dalat, Vietnam, in an old villa on a windblown hill, there surely is still a hole on the wooden floor where the bullet once lodged.
- Strong-willed and feisty, she threw tantrums when she was younger. Hurricane Katrina had nothing on my mother when she was in menopause.
- She once chopped a chicken so hard in anger that its head flew out from the kitchen and bit me on the ankle in the living room. A good fifteen feet. To this day, I am the only person I know who was injured by a dead chicken.
- She was a great storyteller, and people would be mesmerized by the stories she told. And she could change the details mid-sentence so as to have the best effect on the listeners.
- She took the bus every day to go to the convalescent home to visit her mother and mother-in-law in retirement. And she fed them Vietnamese food.
- She would come alive when relatives came to visit. She was happiest when she was with sisters and brothers, children and nieces and nephews. Their joyful laughter often blended in with hers.

• he absolutely adored her grandchildren. She found renewed joy and energy in life in retirement, and she and my father were doting grandparents.

I wish I could share more about my mother but there just isn't enough time.

What I can tell you is this: Alzheimer's slowly took away pieces of my mother until there was nothing left of the once beautiful and vivacious woman.

Yet, as I watched her disappear over the years, I marveled over the miracle that is my mother: even as she forgot who she was, and who I was, she remained true to her nature. Uneaten rice was thrown on the balcony to feed robins and pigeons that made a habit of visiting her each morning. Potted plants died not from neglect but because, well, with no short term memories and bad eyesight, she over watered them—(and eventually we got her plastic orchids, and she, no longer knowing the difference, watered them too and was so proud of how beautifully they bloomed each morning).

A few times, when she could still walk by herself, she disappeared, and this caused my father to panic—but mother had gone around looking for a family of stray cats in the neighborhood that she wanted to feed. So one morning, I accompanied her, and as we walked down the block, I kept thinking: how does someone who forgets where she lives, who struggles to remember her own name, remember that there was a stray cat and her kittens nearby that needed her to feed them?

A passerby may see a thin and frail old woman feeding little kittens, but that was not what I saw. What I saw was the divine expressing itself through those trembling hands that caressed the hungry and the weak. What I saw was the miracle called love made flesh.

And it was sublime.

• • • •

And so . . . all things born must die, ashes to ashes, as they say, dust to dust. Yet ceaselessly, the heavens pour their love into our temporal world, and when manifested through human kindness and compassion, it binds us in a circle of love, and it uplifts and nurtures all beings who suffer.

She did not know it, but all those years ago when my mother cast her spell on my father, its magic also fell on me. In that moment, I knew deep in my heart that I was truly loved, and loved unconditionally, and so I was also free. Free to run far, free to travel the world. Free to fall deeply in love. Free to suffer heartbreaks and self-doubts and failures. Free to triumph. Free to love again.

Because every time I looked back, I'd see my parents standing there over that little boy professing their love. I see the tree of life providing shade.

That magic continues to express itself to this day—and now I wish to share it with all who gathered here to honor my mother's passing, all who descended from her and are bound by kinship and love and kindness, and all who lost loved ones . . . all within the reach of my voice, my words.

First of all, when things get tough, remember to make soup. And, if you can, feed the hungry.

More importantly, open your heart, stand with all your strength, with all your courage for life and living, even in the face of darkness and despair. Despite all your sadness and tears, stand steadfast under that tree and tend to it and watch its branches blossom and bear fruit. Stand until the very last light.

Appreciation

I cannot thank Scott Lankford enough for his encouragement and close reading of my work.

I also want to thank my sister Nancy, who helped me tremendously through the difficult pandemic years.

And I am in profound debt to all the teachers and mentors—Ernest Kaeselau, Michael Rubin, John L'Heureux, Sandy Close, Franz Schurmann, Fenton Johnson, Richard Rodriguez, and many others— whose passion for writing and literature became my own.

I gained much from my maternal grandparents' love for poetry, my father's passion for French literature and philosophy, and my mother's prodigious storytelling gift.

And lastly, to all the lovers who showed me the vast dimensions of my heart, a deep bow in gratitude.

Biographical Note

Andrew Lam fled Vietnam with his family during the fall of Saigon in April 1975 when he was eleven years old. He attended the University of California, Berkeley, studying biochemistry, but abandoned plans for medical school after graduation. He entered the creative writing program at San Francisco State University instead. While still in school, he began writing for Pacific News Service and in 1993 won the Outstanding Young Journalist Award from the Society of Professional Journalists. He has written for many newspapers and magazines since, including *National Geographic Traveler, Los Angeles Times Magazine*, and *The Nation*. A regular commentator on NPR's *All Things Considered* for over seven years, Lam is the author of three books and has won the PEN Open Book Award, the Josephine Miles Literary Award, and many others. He served as a Journalism Fellow at Stanford from 2001 to 2002. In 2004 a PBS documentary about his life called *My Journey Home*, in which a film crew followed him back to Vietnam, was aired nationwide. Lam has lectured at many universities and colleges and taught as a writer-in-residence at San Jose State University from 2015 to 2016. He is working on a novel and a memoir about his childhood in Vietnam during the war.